A Triple Talaq in Kodagu

Ravindran Pottekkat

Foreword and Acknowledgements

This is my fourth book in English and I hope, the readers will accept it with delight. This novel is the story of Kodagu, the picturesque, lush green valley of fragrance, situated in the western ghat ranges. The main protagonist of this novel is Mr.Mohammed Rafeeque, a rich and educated young man, belonging to the Pathan clan. In real life, I've met many such people, at different parts of India. During the Muslim rule, many people from Afghanistan, Iran, Turkey and present Pakistan came to India, to work as soldiers and other officials of the Muslim rulers. Many of them, married from Indian families and made India their home .They are now part and parcel of India. The famous story of Tagore` Kabuliwala ', is still vivid in our memory. Their descendants are found in all states of India, mingled and blended with the local population. The landscape of Afghanistan is really fascinating, but rocky and infertile. The minds of Afghan people also became hard as rock and they are not fed up of decades long war. They are brave, tough and adventurous, but in Mohammed Rafeeque, the hero of this novel, we can see a simple, amiable and god- fearing person. He had done some mistakes, during his formative adolescent and youthful period of life, but in later life, he has proved himself to be a good and generous personality. For all his wrongs, he repents later and goes in search of nirvana or redemption.

The life and culture of Kodavas also have been depicted in this novel. They are friendly, refined, cultured and highly hospitable people. Kodagu is a land of valiant people. They are a martial race and also good farmers. There are some unique characteristics in them, which distinguish them from other sections of people of India. There are many theories and assumptions about their origin. One theory says that they are the descendants of the soldiers of Alexander, the great. According to second theory, Kodava life style and features are similar to that of the Yezidi group, among Kurds of Iraq. Like Zoroastrians, some of them would have escaped to India, fearing conversion to Islam and reached Kodagu. But, no plausible evidence is available to prove such claims. According to the Hindu Purana, a king named Chandra Varma, from the Matsya-Desh, in the North, went on a pilgrimage to the South India, escorted by his soldiers and they came to the source of Cauvery River and was impressed by the beauty and tranquility of the landscape which was lying thinly populated. Chandra Varma felt an infatuation towards this virgin land and they settled down there and became the first Raja of this enchanting and mesmerizing highland. The present population is the descendants of those people who arrived here in the 13th century. Presently, they are an indigenous chivalrous race of Karnataka state. Their language is a mixture of Kannada, Tamil and Malayalam. They are exempt from the Indian Arms Act and can carry guns with them and no license is required. Though they are Hindus, they do not belong to the mainstream of Hinduism They are unique in their culture, lifestyle, customs and cuisine. Their men are tall, fair complexioned and broad headed and women fair and beautiful. Field Marshal Cariappa, Gen. Thimmayya and several other top officers of Indian armed forces belong to this race. They are a dwindling race and constitute only 20 % of the population of Kodagu. They like farming, hunting, adventure, dance and drinks. I hope that I have succeeded in depicting their distinct characteristics and unique lifestyle, in its true perspective.

My first and third books are collections of short stories viz. Infatuation (Character is Destiny) and Old Age Companion. The former is a collection of 18 short stories and the latter, a collection of 10 short stories. The second and fourth works are novels, namely Santhara made him a saint and A Triple Talaq in Kodagu. The Santhara Made Him a Saint is the story of Wayanad which is also a valley of coffee and other spices. The story revolves around a rich Jain planter who was once an atheist and member of Naxalite outfit and later transformed into a devotee of God and found solace in Santhara which is fast unto death, for attainment of moksha or redemption.

The main hero of the novel- A Triple Talaq in Kodagu, is Mohammed Rafeeque, an educated rich planter belonging to Pathan race. The main heroine is Jahanara hailing from an Afghan family. It is difficult to see such a strong willed lady like her in our society. She resembles the Jahanara Begum Sahiba of history. There is a subsidiary heroine by name Saira Bhanu who claims to be a distant relative of Tipu Sultan, is responsible for the Triple Talaq and the subsequent poignant and tragic twist of the story. Rafeeque becomes a sad, reclusive and repentant man, after the death of his wife and second daughter and goes in search of peace of mind through prayer and charity.

I hereby thank my wife Prasanna, daughters Junitha and Thanuja and son- in- laws Sinish Gopi and Sathyajith, for their valuable inspiration, for writing this novel. My special thanks are due to Sinish Gopi who undertook the job of reading the manuscript, editing and uploading the same for publication.

Disclaimer.

The story of this novel and the characters are cent percent fictional and if there is any similarity or resemblance with anybody living or dead, it is purely accidental. To make reading interesting and authentic, real names of some countries, places, institutions and historic characters have been used in this novel, without belittling their values and importance.

Bangalore'   Ravindran Pottekkat
05-01-2019   E.mail - ravindranpg46@gmail.com

Contents

1. Prologue 7

2. Kodagu the valley of fragrance 14

3. Krithika marries Mr. Bopanna. 25

4. Fire at Estate Factory Kotagiri 51

5. Rafeeque divorces Jahanara............................. 68

6. Rafeeque convicted for 5 years 84

7. Jahanara's agony and ecstasy........................... 96

8. The tragic death of Akbar Khan........................111

9. Rafeeque gets his first parole 122

10. Jahanara goes through an ordeal....................136

11. Maj. Devaiah proves his worth 151

12. Jahanara resents reunion................................164

13. Untimely demise of Zeenath 187

14. Epilogue..199

1. Prologue

Kodagu- year 2002

Kodagu is a small picturesque hilly district of Karnataka State in India, lying in the lap of western ghat ranges. It is an enchanting place with mesmerizing hills, gurgling brooks, cascading waterfalls, placid rivers, silent valleys, captivating meadows and verdant forests. Wherever we look, we can see unending luscious greenery and scenic beauty. For centuries, it was a landlocked place, inaccessible for outsiders. It is famous for coffee and a host of other forest products. The climate is very pleasant, since it is situated at a height of 1200 M, above sea level. The people are very refined and hospitable. The original inhabitants of this place is called Kodavas and they have some distinct features and peculiarities when compared to the people of other areas, in Karnataka and India. The males are tall and broad headed and the ladies are tall, fair and beautiful. Kodavas are rich, refined and martial in nature. It is also a famous tourist place. The important tourist places are Nagerhole National Park(Rajiv Gandhi National Park), Talakaveri Temple, which is situated at the source of river Cauvery, at an altitude of 1276M, Kushalnagar, where the famous Buddhist Namdroling monastery is situated and the fourth place is Madikeri where there is a fort , a famous Church built in Gothic style , Omkareshwara Hindu Temple and Tombs of Kodagu Rajas. Madikeri is presently the headquarters of this hill district.

The history and origin of Kodavas are still unknown and shrouded in mystery. They were warriors by profession from time immemorial and also good farmers. They have been permitted to carry arms with them, for self defence. In olden days hunting was their pastime. The whole hills and valleys of Kodagu, except reserve forests, belonged to them. The forests were cleared and coffee and other spices were cultivated, during the time of British rule. Now, it is a rich agricultural and tourist place. In the absence of any proof of their origin, they are considered to be an indigenous race with martial qualities. The Kodavas are the owners of thousands of acres of coffee plantations. According to Kodava history, a large number of their people had been killed during the wars and a sizeable portion of Kodavas converted to Islam and they are called Kodava mappilas. The real Kodava clan remained untouched, by other cultures and civilizations. Many of them have disposed of their lands in Kodagu and moved to Bangalore, Mysore, and Ooty, other cities in India and abroad. The Kodava population in Kodagu is less than two lakhs. Now, we can see planters from all states, belonging to all religious, linguistic and ethnic groups, at this hill station.

It was the middle of January. Thick fog hung in the air, over Kodagu for weeks together. The Golden Valley Estate of Kodagu lay drowsily, under the blanket of fog. It was coffee harvesting season and workers were plucking ripe seeds, in the inclement weather. It was difficult to see one another, due to the presence of thick fog. They spread plastic sheets under the coffee plants and pulled down the seeds from each twig to the sheets below. Due to lack of visibility, they plucked both the green and golden cherries of seeds. The Sun was on its way to the zenith of the sky and it looked like the moon on the full moon day. A chilly wind kept blowing producing a rustling sound. The workers were in sweaters and mufflers and still they shivered in the chill of the morning air. Then, the foggy air began to drizzle and the workers ran in search of shelter leaving the harvested cherry beans to the mercy of rain. It was coffee harvesting season in Kodagu. With the occasional drizzle, new buds had formed on the twigs of coffee plants and a penetrating fragrance emanated from these blossoms and filled the whole valley. Millions of butterflies of various colours and shapes rushed to the valley for pollination of coffee blooms. Thousands of temporary workers had come from different parts of the state, for the work. Makeshift tarpaulin tents have been put up, at different parts of the estate, for their stay.

The Golden Valley Estate has an area of 300 acres and is one of the medium type estates of Kodagu. It is owned by Mr. Mohammed Rafeeque, son of retired Forest Divisional Officer, Rehmatullah Khan. The ancestors of Rehmatullah were in the service of Mysore Raja. They came to Mysore from Kabul, centuries ago. Presently, this property is in the possession of a middle aged lovely lady, named Jahanara. Her husband, Mohammed Rafeeque went to jail for a period of 5 years, in an attempt to murder his wife. A domestic quarrel occurred between Rafeeque and his wife Jahanara and Rafeeque in a fit of anger divorced her by Triple Talaq. Infuriated in this heinous action, Jahanara hit him with a flower vase. He became violent, slapped her on her face several times and also stabbed her in the stomach, with a knife. Jahanara fell down screaming and blood flowed from the wound and drenched her cloths. Rafeeque ran away from the spot in his car. Hearing her cry, the driver and domestic servants rushed to her rescue and she was taken to the hospital, immediately. With the grace of God, she escaped from the jaws of death. The police charged a criminal case against Rafeeque and the court awarded him simple imprisonment for 5 years.

Mohammed Rafeeque has two close friends belonging to the Kodava community, namely Mr. Chengappa and Devaiah. They were members of the Lions Club of Kodagu. Rafeeque met them in a meeting of the club and became close friends. Even though, they belonged to different family environments, they became very close and spent time in discussing regional issues, agricultural problems and political developments. They used to meet frequently in the club for playing rummy and shuttle. They also went to the forest occasionally for taking wild photographs and conducting shikar. Their families met one another once in a year, in the residence of any of them and enjoyed heavy feast with hot drinks.

When Rafeeque was convicted by court, his friends sympathized with him and went to see him. In the jail, twice. After that, Chengappa forgot him completely due to his preoccupations. Devaiah met him accidentally at Ajmer when he visited this shrine, during his first parole. Jahanara took over the charge of two estates viz. the Golden Valley estate, Virajpet and Mariam estate at Hassan. She was very much aggrieved in the Triple talaq slapped on her, but she didn't lose heart and has run the estates boldly and efficiently for years. Much water has flowed through the Cauvery River and her daughters grew up and are now doing house surgeoncy, in the Christian Medical College, Hospital at Bangalore.

Chengappa was recently elected as president of the Coffee Growers Association. He was sitting in his office, discussing with some of the planter friends. Time was about 11.30hrs and it was drizzling outside. A haggard looking man came to the office uninvited and stopped at the door seeing some visitors inside. His face was pale and cheerless, with bristles of grey beard and the lusterless grey strands of hair danced in the breeze. He waited there for about 20 minutes. When the visitors left the office, he got inside and faced his friend Chengappa.

`Chengappa sir, do you remember me? I 'm Rafeeque.' The visitor said feebly.

`Rafeeque. Rafeeque 'Chengappa stood up involuntarily and welcomed him.

`Sir, I'm a free bird now. I've been released from jail.' Rafeeque tried to smile, but his face became grim and pallid.

`Sorry, I could not recognize you, Rafeeque. It is long 5 years after you went inside; please be seated' Chengappa said pointing to a chair in front of him.

Rafeeque sat down and tried to smile again.

`I've nowhere to go in Virajpet. Jahanara will never accept me.' Rafeeque spoke in faint tone.

`Did you have breakfast?'

`No, I came here direct from the jail.'

`Within a few minutes I'll be free and we can go home'

` OK sir, what about your son?'

'He is also in a predicament. I'll tell you everything peacefully. Now, let us go'.

Within 20 minutes, they reached the residence of Chengappa. He called his wife and introduced the newcomer.

'Nina, do you know this fellow? This is Rafeeque, our old family friend. He is coming here after long 5 years. Devaiah is now manager of his estate, at Kotagiri, Ooty.'

'Namaste Rafeeque, we've almost forgotten you.' Nina greeted him with a warm smile on her face.

'Did you go to your house, now? How is Jahanara and children?' Chengappa enquired.

'No, I didn't go there. She'll not accept me. My children are doing house surgeoncy. Devan sir would have told you about my wish for reunion with Jahanara. I came here to seek your help in this issue.'.

'Let us talk peacefully. Please have breakfast; you look tired and weird.'

Rafeeque consumed a lot of idlies and two cups of tea .Chengappa gave him company and after that he was taken upstairs.

'Rafeeque, you can fresh up and rest for some time.'

'OK, thank you.'

After a thorough shave and bath, Rafeeque looked into the mirror and felt elated. He looked young, handsome and energetic. Then, he rested for about two hours in the room, set apart for him. Chengappa waited in the study room. Rafeeque slipped into a shallow snooze. His mind travelled to the good old days of his life about 7 years back. He recollected in a flash, the past events of his turbulent life. Many unexpected and unwanted things had happened in his life. He is always optimistic and is trying to recapture his old life and peace of mind. But, luck did not favour him and the reunion with his old wife did not materialise mainly due to the objection of that lady. At the end he becomes a broken man and goes in search of redemption.

2. Kodagu the valley of fragrance

Kodagu 1995.

Golden valley estate of Virajpet, lay sprawling in the lap of three hills, of the Western Ghats. During spring, the valley will be a sea of yellow, with bright blooms of wild flowers, growing in abundance, everywhere. It will wear a golden mantle during autumn. The leaves of the shade trees will start to dry up with the arrival of this season and the colour of the leaves will change from green to yellow and then pink or golden and the whole valley will lie under a golden canopy. Shortly, the trees will shed their leaves and stand naked looking at the sky, till the arrival of monsoon. Then, the whole valley will again flourish and wear a mantle of dark green. There are plenty of shade trees in the estate, such as silver oak, pine, cedar, teakwood, ebony, rosewood jackfruits etc. The shade trees give shade and coolness to the coffee plants. There is a lovely mansion, in the middle of the estate, with a beautiful garden in front of it and this is the residence of Mohammed Rafeeque. It was constructed by his father, retired Divisional Forest Officer, Rehmatullah Khan, some 5 years ago. Rehmatullah became a multi-millionaire and amassed immense wealth and assets, in Karnataka and Tamil Nadu. After the demise of Rehmatullah and his wife Mariam Beevi, their only son Mohammed Rafeeque assumed charge of the vast empire.

Mohammed Rafeeque is aged 45, height 5' 8'' and of good physique. He is a post graduate from Mysore University. When his father was alive, he had no duties and responsibilities. He enjoyed life by roaming with friends, playing cricket and visiting important sightseeing places of India. He was bold and adventurous and had no regrets in spoiling the life of one of his lady classmates. Rafeeque had taken a girl studying with him in BCom third year to Ooty and freed her after two days. There was huge hue and cry and the Principal had given a police complaint, in this regard since the girl was an inmate of the college hostel. Rahmatullah was in service at that time and he with the help of some top leaders of the state, hushed up the case secretly, by spending a huge amount. No criminal case was registered against him by the police. Her father Revanna who was a planter at Madikeri, later came to know about this incident from the Principal. He became ashamed and depressed, in the disgrace and ignominy of the family and made an attempt to commit suicide. But, he did not succeed in this attempt. With the advice of his wife, he later visited the house of Mr. Rahmatullah Khan and humbly requested him to arrange the marriage of his daughter Krithika with his son Mohammed Rafeeque.

`DFO sir, I'm Revanna, from Madikeri. Your son has spoiled the future of my beloved daughter. I can't keep my tainted daughter in my house. I love her very much and I can't kill her. Let her live anywhere with her lover; I'm prepared to give her in marriage to your son. Please don't say` No' and arrange the marriage, at the earliest.'

`Revanna, your daughter is equally responsible for the incident. It is she who instigated my son for a trip to Ooty and you are putting the whole blame on my son. I'm ready for their marriage, but you should give her 100 acres of coffee estate, as dowry. Can you do that?'

`No DFO sir, there is no dowry system in our community. I'm unable to meet your demand. If you insist, I will give 25 acres of coffee estate and 50 sovereigns of jewellery, for my daughter, as her share. If you reject my request, I'll never come to you again. We Kodavas are not used to giving their daughters in marriage to Muslims, but what to do? The pranks of my daughter has forced me to do such a sacrilege. Your wife is a Kodava mappilas (convert) and hence, I've every right to send my daughter to your house.

`But Revanna, we are Muslims and there is dowry system in our community. I've only one son and he'll get millions as dowry. But, I don't ask that much; I want 100 acres only and you can afford it.' Rehmatullah stuck to his earlier demand.

` I believe in God. You are performing namaz 5 times daily; but I used to go to temple once in a week. Both of us are same before God almighty. You've amassed huge wealth by treachery, muscle power and wickedness. I don't know how to cheat others. I've brought up my children with love and truth. They are unblemished and will have all the virtues of the world. If you cheat me and my family, God will never forgive you. I say you'll be doomed and my curse will trail you and your family forever.' Revanna blurted out with anger and indignation.

Rehmatullah did not reply. He looked really shattered, but was not ready to accept defeat. He remained pensive and silent and looked outside. Revanna realized that Rehmatullah had no interest to talk further and hence he lingered there for about ten minutes and then left the house silently. He was weeping when he walked out of the compound and outside the gate, his son was waiting for him with a bike 'Papa, what did he say?' His son asked when Revanna came out of the gate.

'Rehmatullah did not accept my request. I've not seen such a greedy and inhuman fellow like him. He wanted one hundred acres of coffee estate as dowry, to agree to the marriage.' Revanna   mumbled.
He wiped his tears with a kerchief, sat on the pillion seat of the bike and sped off.

Rehmatullah Khan could not sleep that night. He lay in a reverie and recollected his past. He hailed from a medium type family of Hunsur. His father Ayub Khan was a soldier in the service of Mysore Raja. He had to struggle hard to bring up his three children, Rehmatullah, Feroz and Mansoor. They were living in a tile roofed house, near the Hunsur market. After independence, he lost his job in the Mysore palace and after much efforts, he got another job in a coffee estate at Virajpet, as supervisor. It was owned by a Kodava Muslim called Aboobacker.

Rehmatullah was bright in studies and after matriculation, he was selected as forester and after training got posting at Kuttah range office. Feroz and Mansoor could not complete matriculation and hence left to Bangalore. They worked in a hotel, at K.R. Market as suppliers and later moved to Shivaji Nagar and joined a furniture shop as helpers, on daily wage basis. Ayub Khan's wife Sabnam Beevi was a pious lady and she had no ambitions in life and spent time in domestic chores and prayers.

Rehmatullah was smart and courageous. One day, he was deputed by his boss to catch a gang who was stealing sandalwood trees from the forest? He was accompanied by two guards and one forest watcher. They reached the spot where about fifty medium type sandalwood trees were growing and concealed the jeep behind a tree, about 500 M away. They hid themselves in a thicket and waited for the sandalwood thieves. At 2 am, they heard a feeble scratching sound of saw cutting the sandalwood tree. Rehmatullah and party moved in the direction of the trees and saw three thieves cutting the tree with an electric saw. They were fully armed. Rehmatullah saw the thieves in the torch light. Suddenly, they heard the crackle of a gun. Instantly, Rehmatullah fell down and blood flowed profusely from his shoulder. The thieves ran in different directions leaving the saw and weapons behind. The forest officers ran behind them, but could not catch any of them. The thieves were very familiar with the terrain and escaped by that time. They came back, recovered the saw and the weapons from the thicket and went in search of Rehmatullah. He was lying in a pool of blood in a serious condition and they carried him to their jeep and sped to Virajpet government hospital, immediately. The doctors applied first aid and stopped the flow of blood. He lay there, in a semi-conscious state. At the crack of dawn, DFO and other officers reached the hospital and met the doctors and pressed them to retrieve the bullet from the body of the patient. He was immediately operated on and the bullet was taken out. When he was lying in the hospital, his bapa and his boss Aboobacker came to see him. He lay in bed for about one week and got discharged. Even though, the sandalwood thieves were not brought to book, the department decided to give out of turn promotion to Rehmatullah, for his devotion to duty and bravery. Later, his bapa's boss Aboobacker decided to give his second daughter Mariam to Rehmatullah and the same was accepted with great joy and ecstasy by Ayub Khan and family. He got 50 acres of coffee estate as dowry and 50 sovereign jewellery in this marriage. His wife Mariam was a tall and fair lady with average beauty, wisdom and education.

After marriage, Rehmatullah was promoted as Ranger and on successful completion of the training, posted at the range office, Chamarajanagar. This was the beginning of his luck and sudden opulence of the family. One day, he stopped a lorry with full of Teakwood, without any gate pass. The lorry was seized and the driver and cleaner were taken into custody. Within half an hour, the local MLA and his goons arrived on the spot and threatened Rahmatullah with dire consequences. The MLA Puttaswamy pulled his collar and shouted.

`Heh Ranger, what is your name? Who posted you here? I 'm the local MLA and without my orders you can't seize a lorry in my area. I say you haven't seized this lorry and taken the driver into custody. The lorry stopped at this check post is free to go'. The MLA ordered.

The driver came forward and started the lorry and left the spot. Rehmatullah and his staff returned to the office, in anger and indignation.

`Is this range the property of this MLA?' Rehmatullah asked his assistants.

`Sir, he is very powerful and close with the ministers of forest and home. If we didn't obey, they will make our lives miserable.

About 2 years back, one Ranger named Vasudev refused to execute his orders in a similar case. He was abducted and after two days, his mutilated body was recovered from the forest with a big hole in his stomach.

The police registered a case and the same was closed with report that the death was unnatural. Investigations have revealed that the officer was attacked by a wild elephant, while he was on duty and got killed with its tusk.' One guard told him.

`Then, why didn't you tell me about it, when I took charge of this range?'

`We thought you are aware of this problem'

`In Kuttah, there was no such problem. We had threats from poachers and sandalwood thieves and their menace was crushed recently.'

`Sir, there is another vampire. Have you heard of forest brigand Ponnappan? He is a ruthless man with many followers. He is a threat for Tamil Nadu as well as Karnataka. He is active in Sathyamangalam range and will come to our area also, occasionally for shooting elephants and cutting sandalwood trees.'

Rehmatullah was oblivious of the various dangers lurking in the forest and was very careful while dealing with poachers and sandalwood thieves. All of them had goons and godfathers in politics. In addition to this, they have to face encroachers of forest land. Reserve forests are safe since there are stringent rules to protect it. In the contiguous forest land, there are thousands of encroachments and they are fighting for title deeds, through politicians. They will allow people to put up temporary tents in such lands by accepting money. If the media and press report such cases, they will put the blame on forest officials. He became afraid and suspicious of the loyalty of his own subordinates.

One day, Rehmatullah was preparing food in his quarter and he heard a commotion outside. He came out of the house and was confronted by a dark tall man with a rifle slung over his shoulder. About ten people with guns escorted him.

'Heh Officer, I'm Ponnappan, Sathyamangalam Ponnappan. I came here to see the new Ranger. All the previous officers were very obliging and I hope you also will be like that. If you don't cooperate, the consequences will be terrible. We'll give you a handsome amount every month. You can tell me if you have any difficulties to work with us. Don't hesitate to tell me, if the monthly payment is less. Don't pass on information about our movements to the higher ups. Don't try to stop our work, don't try to counter us or betray us. If you have any requests or demands you are free to tell me. If you are obliging, we'll help you and protect you in every way possible.' Ponnappan said.

'Bhayya we've no complaints; we are happy here.' Rehmatullah replied in fear.

'There is an unseen rule here which every-body has to observe. You do not see anything, you do not hear anything and you do not say anything, understand.' He roared.

Rehmatullah was afraid to say anything and he stood smiling at the marauders. Then, one of them fired a shot at the top of a tree. All birds perched on the tree, flew away in fear, with a sudden thud. After lingering for about ten minutes, they walked away in long strides.

Rehmatullah was really terrified. For the first time in his life, he became very much scared and anxious about his life. After that incident, he always took a forest watcher and guard and kept a rifle with him while going to the forest, for inspection. In due course, he became an obedient servant of Ponnappan and thereby acquired enough courage and self-confidence. With the passage of time, he became very close with Ponnappan and thereby he became very bold and ruthless.

One night, Ponnappan came to his quarters with two comrades and spoke to him for about one hour. He appeared very friendly and amiable. Rahmatullah prepared tea and served to him and his comrades.

`Sir, we are engaged in some illegal activities. The political masters are demanding more and more money. I'm taking risks myself and risking the lives of my faithful comrades. To break law or do illegal things is not a simple thing. Others are sitting in air conditioned rooms and demanding more and more. Many officers from forest, police and revenue departments have tried to catch me and my boys alive. For saving our lives we have killed and maimed a lot of people. It was not intentional and we sincerely sympathise with the families of those unlucky people. If you want timber just tell me and I'll give truckloads of teak wood or ebony or sandalwood. My people have auctioned forest coups here and in Tamil Nadu. You ask your brother to start a timber business and within a short period he will become rich. If you have any unemployed brothers please ask them to take some risks and they can mint money and become millionaire, overnight. No investment is required and what is required is courage and self-confidence. '

Sandalwood is in great demand in Bangalore. Let him start an agency of Ayurveda medicines and I'll supply sandalwood and ivory. Just think over it and help me in my endeavour. He gave a cover to Rehmatullah but he declined. Ponnappan kept the cover on the teapoy and left the quarters, after wishing goodnight.

Rehmatullah was frightened out of his wits and he heaved a sigh of relief when he left. He opened the cover with trembling hands. It contained an amount of Rs 2000/- and he was baffled. He looked again and again at the crisp 100 rupee notes and he could not believe his eyes. The whole night his mind told him to return the money to Ponnappan, but finally his mind advised him to be practical and take the money as gift and get rid of the guilty feeling. Rehmatullah learned all formalities, tricks and treacheries of his profession and shone as Ranger and then as Forest Divisional Officer. He was very careful and protected himself from unnatural death, till retirement, from the unseen dangers like wild animals, poachers, sandalwood thieves, contractors, mafias, superiors, subordinates and politicians.

After the marriage of Rahmatullah, his father Ayub Khan, quit the job in his father- in- law's estate and started a timber mill, near Gundlupet. His brothers Feroz and Mansoor started an Ayurveda medical shop at Shivaji Nagar. Day by day, the family of Rahmatullah began to prosper and within a short period they became millionaires. Rehmatullah amassed immense wealth and purchased three plots of land on the main road, Mysore and constructed a palatial residential building at Hunsur. Feroz and

Mansoor started various other business enterprises in Bangalore city, MG Road and Frazer town and became multi-millionaires. They constructed two big residential houses at Shivaji Nagar and married from rich and influential families.

Ayub Khan and his wife lived with Rehmatullah and his family at Hunsur, till their death. Feroz and Mansoor gradually rose in society as big businessmen and religious leaders. They got support from political circles and got license for many educational institutions.

@@@@@@@

3. Krithika marries Mr. Bopanna.

Revanna had one son and two daughters and he had only 200 acres of coffee plantation as property. Hence, he could not agree to the demand of Rehmatullah. By that time, a marriage proposal came for Krithika. The groom was a widower and had 50 acres of coffee and an old house at Kushalnagar. Revanna later, gave her in marriage to this man aged 42 with 2 school going sons. After BCom, Mohammed Rafeeque joined MCom in the same college and came out successful. He did not apply for any job and started assisting his father in the estate affairs. Also, he worked in a Tutorial college at Mysore for one year. Jahanara was a student there and he liked her, proposed and married. After his marriage with Jahanara, Mohammed Rafeeque became a bit sober. His wife Jahanara also hailed from an Afghan family and had all the shrewdness and astuteness required for taming her husband. He really feared her and her brothers and he pretended to be an obedient husband. His devotion in the running of the estates was appreciated by his wife. After the demise of his parents, Rafeeque became very charismatic and reasonable in his perception and attitude towards his family and the world around him. He entertained a guilty feeling, in the unceremonious treatment, meted out to his lover, Krithika. Also, he regretted sincerely, in the humiliation of her father by his father. Once, he heard a terrible news from his college mate Avinash, after many years that Krithika was pregnant at the time of her marriage. She agreed for the marriage to save her father from a second suicide attempt. On the first night itself, she told her husband that she was carrying.

He was devastated and wept like a child, the whole night. Next day, he did not show any anxiety or worry on his face and consoled Krithika.

`I'll keep this secret in my mind till my death. You should look after my children. They are only fledglings and can't live without a mother. You should be a mother to them' Bopanna said.

`Your children are my children and I'll love and look after them more than my child.' Krithika assured him.

Krithika gave birth to a lovely baby boy with sparkling eyes and fair complexion and he was named as Ashik. Bopanna brought him up along with his other sons Nirmal and Nanda who were in 10th standard. One night, Bopanna went out with his gun to shoot wild boar causing damage to his plantain trees.

That night, he did not come back. Krithika became aghast and terrified. She went out with her sons in the dark, in search of her husband; but could not locate him .Her sons called out loudly in the pitch darkness but nobody answered. They searched with the aid of a torch the plantain grove and surroundings, but in vain. When they were returning, they heard the howling of a wolf at a distance. Some wild boars ran around them frantically, making a moaning sound. They were scared and returned to the house in terror and grief. She and her sons waited sleeplessly, the whole night, for their papa. Next day, her brothers were called in and during the search operations, Bopanna's lifeless body was discovered in a ditch, near the plantain grove with an injury at his temple.

Many years rolled by and Bopanna's sons grew up. Bopanna's son Nanda became an Army Officer and Nirmal, a Flying Officer.

They got quick promotion and Nanda is now Lieutenant Colonel and Nirmal Flight Lieutenant. After many years, the third son Ashik completed his LLB and became an Advocate in Virajpet court under Adv. Muthanna. Ashiq, later became the son- in- law of Devaiah.

Mohammed Rafeeque was a voracious eater. His menu consisted of dates, apple, pomegranate, chapatti, egg, goat meat and liver. He wanted to maintain his youthfulness, virility and libido forever. Jahanara trusted him and never had any suspicion in the fidelity of her husband. His main exercise was walking and he used to cover a minimum distance of 10 KMs, along the main road, daily.

One day, after returning from the estate, he called his wife to the porch and discussed many things about their Livingston Estate at Kotagiri, Ooty.

`Jahanara, our Kotagiri estate is running on loss. We've to find out ways and means to make it profitable. The workers are demanding higher wages. The factory is very old and modernization of the machinery is highly necessary. The price of tea has slumped in recent times. How can we make up the loss? Money has to be siphoned from our coffee estates to that estate to tide over the present crisis 'Mohammed Rafeeque said.

`To siphon money from one estate to the other is not advisable. Too much money is lavished every month. You go there and stay in the estate bungalow for two weeks. Don't worry about coffee estates. I can manage these estates, in your absence. Tighten up the expenditure at Kotagiri and increase production. That is the only solution for the present predicament. Don't trust the manager fully and always keep an eye on him? Verify whether tea is locally sold from the factory.

Mohammed Rafeeque liked the suggestion of his wife and he complimented her.

`You are really Jahanara Begum Sahiba of history. Can you work as manager of Livingston Estate, Kotagiri, near Ooty ? Then, it'll run profitably.'

`Who is Jahanara Begum?'

`You are very poor in the history of Mughal empire .She is the eldest daughter of the Emperor Shahjahan. Her brothers were Dara Shikoh and Aurangzeb. Dara Shikoh was the crown prince, but Aurangzeb murdered him and captured power, after imprisoning his father Shahjahan. The great Mughal Emperor, Shahjahan spent his last days looking at the Taj Mahal, through the window of his prison. Really, Jahanara was the rightful heir to the throne, since she was the eldest and able in many ways. After the murder of Dara Shikoh, she became scared and fled from the palace to Himalayas and lived in disguise for many years. The king of Garhwal gave asylum to Jahanara and kept this a secret. The crown prince of Garhwal, betrayed his father for some personal gains from the Mughal Emperor. He informed Aurangzeb about the presence of Jahanara in Garhwal. This news infuriated Aurangzeb and he sent some soldiers to Garhwal to capture her. The Garhwal Raja came to know about this, through his spies and he sent his army to the ghat section of the road, immediately. They destroyed the small army of Aurangzeb, by dropping big size rocks from the top of the mountain, when they were climbing through the ghat road.

Then, he shifted Jahanara to an unknown place under another kingdom and Aurangzeb could not touch her, till her death.'

'I've no knowledge about these Mughal emperors. I 'm only a village maiden, even though my ancestors belong to the same place from where Babur came to India.'

'Can you go to Ooty Kotagiri, to set right things in our estate, there?'

'That is not necessary. You control Mr. Cherian properly and then things will change, overnight. This is only due to lack of proper supervision, control and monitoring.'

' Anyway, I 'm going there shortly .Your suggestions and ideas will be put into practice with a strong hand.'

'It is a wonderful estate and bapa got it for a thrown -away price. It is really a big asset. It can be used for tourism purpose also. Construct a resort deep inside the estate, on the side of mountain. It'll attract a lot of tourists.' Jahanara said.

'I thought of disposing of the estate. If we get a good price that will be better. Otherwise, we should relocate to Kotagiri.'

'I can't live in that horrible climate and freezing cold.'

Mohammed Rafeeque patted his wife warmly and went to meet his friends.

'Jahanara, we have decided to go for a shikar to Nagerhole forest. Chengappa and Devaiah are also coming with me.'

'You'll be caught by the ranger and party. Now, poaching is a serious crime. Don't take unnecessary risk. If you kill a deer or wild boar it will be treated as murder and is a big un-bailable criminal offence. I'll not allow that.' Jahanara warned Rafeeque.

`Jahanara, this is India. If you've money, nobody will touch you. Over and above, I'm the son of DFO, Rehmatullah. My father is dead and gone and still the forest officials shudder in the very mention of his name. Most of these policemen and forest officials are very corrupt. They'll extort money from the poachers and wood mafias and they'll let them free after arrest. The forest officials are hand in glove with these mafias. Forest brigand Ponnappan has killed hundreds of elephants and sold their tusks. He and his gang have cut thousands of sandalwood trees from the forest with the connivance of forest officials and politicians. Many top ranking politicians and forest officials of two states are in his payroll. For catching him, the governments of Karnataka and Tamil Nadu have spent a lot of money. In this endeavour, many brilliant forest and police officers had lost their lives and still he remained elusive and caused menace to the people and governments. Only small flies will be trapped in their nets, but big flies and maggots will break the net and escape. Here, anybody can be purchased. Kite will never fly over money. If anybody dared, he is finished. Hence, nobody will dare to burn his fingers.' Rafeeque made a lecture.

Chengappa was Group Manager of Brookfield Plantations, Ooty. He was a very efficient and able Officer. He was tall and handsome. After completing 25 years of service, he had a fight with his boss about the tea auction. The boss was waiting for an opportunity to sack him. He had submitted resignation letter to the company while receiving appointment order. He joined Eli-stone estate as Asst. Manager and after 12 years, resigned as Sr.

Manager and joined the Brookfield Bros as Group Manager. He was of a proud nature and will never tolerate coercion, bossism and indignity. He is clean, strict and over and above very friendly with the staff. He did everything possible for the workers and this quality was not relished by the top Management. Chengappa's service was terminated by accepting the undated resignation letter submitted by him, many years age.

 Chengappa used to say to his friends ` I'll never send my children to this job. The other managers will kneel if they were asked to sit, but, I'm of a different breed. I 'm not prepared to surrender before anybody. He had enough self-confidence, grit and determination. He left the job without making any appeal to the Management to reconsider their decision. After going home, he took the reins of his estate. He had 700 acres of coffee plantation, at Virajpet. His wife Nina is a postgraduate and is an adept in running coffee plantations. She hailed from a rich planter family of Kuttah. She was running the estate, in his absence. His eldest son is a doctor in US and daughter given in marriage to a businessman, in Bangalore.

The second friend was Mr. Devaiah. He was a retired major in the Indian army. He had actively participated in the Bangladesh war. After graduation, he joined the service, on short service commission and had to retire from service, after the war. He is very bold and adventurous. During the war he was leading a section of Mukti- bahini in the garb of a Bengali, in dhoti and white shirt. He was very rich and had more than 800 acres of coffee estate and 100 acres of paddy field. His wife Nimmi hailed from a rich family of Madikeri. She had some connection with the famous Kodandera family of Madikeri. He gets a lot of money every year, by leasing his fields, for ginger cultivation. Every year, hundreds of people come from Wayanad to Kodagu, for ginger cultivation. The fields are given on lease for one year at the rate of Rs 5000/- per acre. Every year, he gets lakhs of rupees by way of rent. He has three children, viz. two boys and one girl. The boys have completed graduation and are helping their father in the estate work. The girl is youngest and is studying for degree at Mysore.

Rahmatullah Khan, the father of Rafeeque was a tough officer and his juniors as well as seniors were afraid of him. For the contractors and staff he was a terror. He made immense wealth by helping contractors and timber merchants. When he was Ranger, he had allowed four to five loads of timber on one gate pass. Also, under his patronage, prohibited woods such as teak, ebony, sandalwood etc. were allowed to be felled and transported. He got millions in these transactions. He invested this money in lands. His family was living in a small tile roofed house, at Hunsur when he joined the service. Now his son is multi-millionaire. Nobody knew much about his origin and family. It is believed that he is a Pathan. His ancestors came to Mysore and joined the army of Tipu and later Wadiyars. Rahmatullah had another coffee estate of 150 acres at Hassan, adjacent to the forest and a big tea estate of 800 acres at Kotagiri, Ooty. Mohammed Rafeeque was his only son and he passed away two years back and Rafeeque became the sole owner of all the three estates. His mother Mariam Beevi was a very devout and religious lady and she died a couple of months ago. She hailed from a Kodava Muslim family and her two brothers are living in Kuttah. One of her brothers had married from a Muslim family of Kannur, Kerala and the other brother from an Iran family of Shivaji Nagar.

Mohammed Rafeeque and Jahanara had two children, both girls, named Rabia and Zeenath and they are studying for +1 at a convent school at Bangalore. Jahanara is a strong lady and she hailed from Mysore. Her father Usman Haji and brothers Jaleel and Nazar are doing hardware business in Mysore town. They are financially well off and have enough landed properties at Mysore and Gundlupet. Jaleel and Nazar were members of a mafia gang. They used to achieve many things through muscle power and organized crime. They had many boys with them to take up any kind of mission. Jahanara also has acquired some toughness from her brothers. But, their father Usman was very pious and observed the rules of the religion strictly and performed namaz 5 times, daily. He never deposited money in banks since he was against interest. He had constructed many small type houses in Mysore and given them for rent. He has many bank accounts and the interests received will be given away to the poor during the holy month. Usman has gone to Haj three times and once he had taken his wife also with him.

Mohammed Rafeeque is an ideal farmer. Every day, he used to go to the estate and cover long distance over hills and dales. He used to visit the Hassan estate once in every week .This estate is situated on the boundary of Hassan district with Chikmagalur district and is a forest area. The estate is surrounded by thick forests and wild animals including elephants used to enter the estate and make extensive damage to the crops. Elephants come in herds and destroy plantain, coconut saplings and jackfruit trees. They like jackfruits and during season they will come in herds and pluck its fruits and eat lavishly, after crushing them with their foot. No managers have been posted for these two coffee estates, but in the Tea estate at Ooty, two Managers, two Ass.t Managers and one PRO have been appointed. His estate has an area of 800 acres covering three mountain chains, along Kotagiri road. The hill side of this estate is dotted with quarters of the workers. It originally belonged to an Englishman called Ralph.

Mr. Ralph was the Customs Officer in Madras (present Chennai) for about 7 years. He was very strict and straightforward in his dealings. He was the only son of his parents and they stayed in a big house on the banks of Thames. His father Nicholas was a sailor for long 15 years. He became fed up with sea life and retired from service at the age of 35 after completing 15 years of service. He married Dorothy after his retirement. Dorothy was a school teacher and was 10 years junior to him. After the birth of Ralph, Nicholas started a laundry near their house and life was happy and harmonious, till Ralph completed his graduation. He was adventurous and had great ambition and enthusiasm to visit foreign countries and explore unknown lands. Hence, he decided to become captain of a ship. But, his father discouraged him and finally consented for an assignment in India, in 1938. He joined the customs department in Chennai and after 5 years appointed as Customs Superintendent. He captured many smuggling vessels and one day he was attacked by some unknown assailants. He was seriously injured and spent about three months in hospital.

Ralph was granted one month leave after discharge from hospital and he set sail to England. His parents were very happy in the arrival of Ralph. They compelled him to remain in England and spend a peaceful life after getting married. But, his mind was in Madras. Hence, he invited his parents to travel with him to Madras. They were not willing to leave England and hence Ralph sailed to India alone. After joining duty, he fell ill again and hence he was sent to Ooty for a change of environment. He used to go to the English club daily and there he happened to meet one retired police officer by name Livingston. He was running a tea estate at Kotagiri after voluntary retirement from service at the age of 35, when he was police commissioner of Madras. Now, he is above 60 and wanted to take his wife to England for treatment. Ralph purchased the estate from Livingston and he resigned his job at Madras and became a full time planter. Ralph learned Tamil and spent his prime youth in the management of his estate. Ralph brought his parents to India and they spent about three months in the estate bungalow and then returned to England. After independence, most of his friends returned to England, but he remained here for some more time. Nobody turned up to purchase the estate since it is a labour oriented Industry. Rahmatullah came to know about this estate through a friend and he got it for a low price. After disposal of his estate, Ralph returned to England and joined his family.

After purchasing the Livingston Tea estate, Rahmatullah spent a lot of money for modernization of the factory, office and quarters of workers.They had a school, hospital and co-operative society within the premises of the estate. The major portion of the staff and workers were Tamils. The roads inside the estate were also bituminized. After retirement, Rehmatullah personally supervised the running of the estate. The plucked chap (leaves) were processed in their factory .The processed tea was disposed of by auction in Chennai. Representatives of foreign countries will come to Chennai for auction at regular intervals and thus tea stock was disposed of by auction at regular intervals of time.

After the demise of Rahmatullah, Mohammed Rafeeque began to visit Kotagiri estate once in a week. Manager was Mr. Cherian and Asst. Managers Sundaram and Thirunavakarasu helped Manager Cherian in day- today- affairs of the estate. PRO Ramaswamy was in charge of public dealings and labour problems. Whenever the proprietor arrived, the main bungalow will be opened for his stay. A cook will be employed temporarily, to prepare food for Rafeeque, till his return to Virajpet.

There is a UP school, dispensary and leaf (chap) processing factory in the estate. Up to UP level the children of workers can study in this school. After this, they can join the government school in the Kotagiri town or the missionary English medium school. Like Coonoor and Ooty, Kotagiri is also a beautiful tourist place and there are many tourist spots, there. Throughout the year, the whole landscape will be in blooms.There are many important sightseeing places at this place such as Kodanad view point, Catherine falls, Ekk falls, Rallia dam , Lamb's rock, Sim's park etc. Rafeeque used to visit these places and spend blissful hours there. It is a gift of the Nature and the ambience one gets at this location is glorious and indescribable. It is a quiet and enchanting place. It is really a tourist paradise.

Mohammed Rafeeque usually stayed at a hotel named Paradise and indulged in wine and women. He'll pay a visit to the Tea Estate and then withdraw to the coziness of the hotel. He had some friends there who'll arrange high society ladies for him. He is prepared to pay any amount for this revelry. He knew that Kotagiri is a quiet and safe place for his pleasure hunt and nobody of his relatives or friends will come to know about it. His manager Cherian knew about it, but he would never divulge this to any of his staff. There is a beautiful estate bungalow in his estate, but he stays there only one day. After discussing the estate problems, he will retreat to his paradise hotel.

At his home in Kodagu, Rafeeque is of a gentle and amiable disposition and behaves like an ideal fellow. His father was very rude and rough to his workers and supervisors, but Rafeeque was friendly in nature and he was loved and respected by all. There are about 26 workers and two supervisors in his estate at Virajpet. Since it was a coffee estate, only few workers were required. They were used for adding manure to the coffee and other crops and for doing maintenance works in the estate .In some estates ginger will be cultivated in the gap between coffee plants. There are plenty of shade trees such as silver oaks, jackfruits, areca, cedar etc. in the estate. For plucking seeds regular workers are not used. For harvesting work, seasonal workers from other parts of the state are employed, for a period of two months. They come from all parts of Karnataka and outside during December and go back after the harvest, with a handsome amount of money. They'll be provided with free accommodation and food till the plucking work is over. The drying and stocking work is entrusted to the regular workers. For curing of beans they have to be taken to the curing mills.

Usually big companies such as Nestle, Podar, and Cadbury etc will come and collect the seeds without curing process. Most of the curing mills and coffee collecting centers were run by Malayalees.

Rafeeque and family were invited to the house of Chengappa for the annual Kailpodh festival (Festival of arms). Rafeeque attended the ceremony with Jahanara. There were a lot of guests including Devaiah and his family. Most of them were in their traditional attire; black coat with sleeves cut short at the elbow, pants reaching up to the knees, silver sheathed ornate dagger, a scarlet gold sash and gilted turban. The dress of the ladies was very fascinating and they wore sari in a peculiar style and the pleats of sari tucked in at the back of the waist and pinned to the right side. There was a black shawl on the back reaching up to the knee, attractive brooch and jewellery. After the religious rites and rituals including handing over a gun by the eldest member of the family to the elder member of the house, there was sumptuous feast with rice, vegetable curry, fish curry, chicken and pork curry and payasam (dessert). After the feast, men and women started to dance together, a very vibrant and energetic dance. Rafeeque and Jahanara also participated in the dance and merry making. They grew tired very early and settled down in chairs in the porch. Then, Chengappa approached them and enquired `Rafeeque and madam how was the feast?'

`Superb! '

`Our people like pork curry very much. I know you won't take it. Since chicken and fish were served, there was no cause for embarrassment. Did you feel bad?'

`The dishes were very tasty and hence we consumed too much.' Rafeeque said.

`Your costumes are very colourful.' Jahanara remarked.

`Rafeeque, this is our traditional dress. Our community has some special customs and traditions. When a child is born one shot is fired to the sky to greet and welcome the newcomer. When one dies two shots will be fired in quick succession to say adieu to the departed soul. For marriage, the bridegroom will come in martial attire with dagger and sword and do some symbolic acts of mock warfare. He'll cut some plantain stumps and it shows the bridegroom has to win over his opponents to marry the girl.' Chengappa said in a conceited way.

`It is a good practice. In North India, the bridegroom will come on horse with sword and shield. It is obvious that your origin is from the North. We are from Afghanistan or the North West frontier province. After settling in the south, we've given up our customs and traditions long back. We are now living as Kannadigas. Our ladies use only sari or churidar. We used to visit the masjid only for festivals. We have no connection with the local Muslim community here, since we are living among Kodavas.'

`By living among Hindus you have almost imbibed our qualities and food habits also. You are highly refined people, but local population is still orthodox.'

`Absolutely, by the by, I invite you for a picnic in the forest, near Nagerhole National park, on next Friday. 'Rafeeque said.

`OK, I'm ready. Please speak to Devaiah also.'

On the next Friday evening, Rafeeque took his friends, to Nagerhole forest in his jeep. They took with them a big tiffin carrier full of fried chicken, banana chips, and one bottle of Scotch whisky, one bottle of rum, soda bottles and drinking water. They went to a hillock near the gate of the National park and settled on the grass bed. It was a pleasant evening and the Sun had started to descend to the horizon painting the sky with yellow and purple. They spent about four hours eating, drinking and talking.

Chengappa was the first to break silence.

`Rafeeque, I was dismissed from service for no fault of mine. The only fault I did was that, I did not show more respect to our Director, Surendranath Jain. One day, he asked me bluntly - how many tons of tea are balance with you now?'

`The whole quantity has been sent for auction.' I said.

`I don't trust you. I heard that you are selling tea, locally' Jain said.

`No sir, I'm your obedient servant. I've no vested interests in the company affairs '. Said Chengappa.

`How much quantity has been sent for auction?' Director asked.

` 30 tons '

`I 'm not satisfied with your reply. You may proceed on long leave.'

`Long leave? I've not made any request for long leave.'

`I meant that your services are no longer required for our company. Your resignation has been accepted.'   Saying this he put down the receiver.

I could not protest or complain. They had collected an undated resignation letter from me at the time of joining duty. They would have accepted it after marking the date. Their rude behaviour did not affect me. Although I felt a ping in my heart, I was cheerful and talkative as before.

I was given a warm send off by my staff and workers and I returned to my home, after two days in anguish and anger. This is the culture of big companies and corporates. It is really nauseating and disgusting.' Chengappa said in great indignation.

`Chengappa, what I heard is a different version. You'd an affair with the wife of the company doctor. I think he'd complained to the Director for taking action against you. Is it correct?' Devaiah said.

`It is not correct. It is true that I'd some affairs with the wife of the doctor. But, he is innocent or he is not aware of this. Somebody else in the office, would have reported the matter to the management.' Chengappa said.

`I'm innocent in this regard. We were close family friends. One day, Dr. John had gone to Coimbatore. The maid and watchman were on leave. She had a giddiness and she called me to help. I went there immediately with a private doctor. After that, I'd to go there again with medicines and she asked me to remain there, till her husband returned home. She felt a ping in the chest and she asked me to rub her chest and back. In the initial stage, I tried to restrain my passions and controlled myself but in a fit of emotions, we forgot everything .In such a situation, we can't control ourselves? She was really insane due to love and lust. It seemed that she had excessive sex desire. How can I describe it? It was unfathomable and insatiable. She was fire, passion, laughter and tears. She'll spiral me to great heights of physical and mental satisfaction. Really, I was lifted to the heaven and oblivious of everything around us and we lay there hugging each other, for hours together. Her white complexion, sensuous lips and dreamy eyes haunted me. It is difficult to see such a marvellous and sweet woman like her in this world. After that incident, she used to call me frequently. She was usually moody and reclusive. But, in my presence she was really ecstatic, cheerful and boisterous. She used to exult very much in my presence. Some ladies are over sexy and passionate like her. Our relationship continued for quite a long time. I can't forget her. She is such a loving companion. She had given me blissful and unforgettable moments in life. I'd a guilty conscience, but she had none. She loved her husband as before and led a peaceful family life. She is so sweet and intimate. But, god is always jealous and will not allow such relationship forever. After I left that company, she was in such an emotional conflict and was laid up for months. Finally, for a change of environment, Dr. John resigned from service and went to their native place, Wayanad and started practising at Mananthavady town' Chengappa narrated the story.

`Did you go there to meet her again?' Rafeeque was inquisitive.

`No, I never went to her house at Mananthavady which is very near to Kuttah, where my wife house is situated. She is a sweet woman and I can't forget her. Once she had called me, but I didn't give any further hope. My wife Nina is very sincere and loving. I still keep a guilty feeling for having cheated her. If she got a hint of this story, I'm afraid, she will commit suicide. It was a mistake, but I had no control over my body and conscience, in those days. '

`Chengu, you've spoiled one family' Devaiah said.

`Never, they are living very cordially as ideal couple. Sex aberrations have not affected their family life, adversely. Their elder daughter has completed her house surgeoncy and is going to marry a Hindu boy from Thrissur, Kerala .They have no such problems or religious fanaticism.'

`Then, it is well and good. I know such things in many ideal families.' Devaiah said.

`What is life if there is no such adventures? We can't be cent percent perfect. Majority of the ladies are not satisfied with one man. 'Rafeeque said.

Maj. Devaiah narrated his wartime experiences. ` We were deep inside East Bengal. Our Colonel Sab was a Sikh, with exceptional courage and he had cut off his hair to look like a Pathan. The Pakistani soldiers were very cruel and lusty .They shot even boys suspecting them as informers. We could save many young girls from their custody and most of them Hindu and Christian .They were defeated on all fronts and finally surrendered to Indian Army. More than 90,000 soldiers and officers laid down their arms and surrendered. I was a witness to this surrender ceremony. Our Company commander was a Sikh, Brigade commander a Muslim, Corps commander a Jew, Chief of Eastern Command a Sikh and Chief of Army Staff a Parsi. We fought bravely as if we belonged to a single community. This is the success of Indian army, unity in diversity. My ancestors have saved enough for many generations. When they were alive I was a free bird and enjoyed life in the army. In my opinion, all people should undergo army training. Then they will know what is life and the value of discipline. The reason for our present state of affairs is due to lack of discipline. For peace and prosperity, we should learn the value of discipline. While we were in barracks in India, away from families, some of the subordinates were not like me. They used to go in search of pleasure outside to Sonaganj brothel and few of them had contracted venereal diseases.' Devaiah said.

`My case is different. I'd premarital and post -marital sex with a lot of ladies. The Kotagiri is really a pleasure hub. We'll get any type of high society girls, there. For some ladies, it is a pleasure hunt and some others use it for settling scores with their husbands. Nowadays, nobody will do this work for the sake of livelihood. The standard of living has improved a lot and there is no such poverty, anywhere in India. ' Rafeeque said.

`Is it free social service or shall we pay remuneration for their service?' Chengappa was a jovial fellow and he asked in humor. `There is nothing free in this world. The hotel people will charge minimum of Rupees ten thousand for one day service and they may give some three thousand to the lady and meet her cab charges. She'll be satisfied with a pocket money. The hotel owners will take major share of the money, since they have a lot of risks. They've to pay to the staff, police and various other agencies, to avoid unnecessary raids and cases'. Rafeeque elaborated.

`Does your wife have any suspicion about you?' Devaiah enquired.

`Not at all. She is an innocent lady and have no suspicion about my fidelity. I don't tell her any of my adventures' Rafeeque waxed eloquent.

`I trust my wife and she in turn trusts me. It is not proper to break the code of conduct. If we show infidelity, the family life is gone. I'll be faithful to my wife forever. Recently, I read the biography of Field Marshal Cariappa. He and Gen Thimmayya hailed from the famous Kodandera family of Madikeri. Cariappa's son Nanda was Air Marshal and daughter Nalini a homemaker. He was a workaholic and spent most of his time in his office. He was always busy with his duties and had no time to give special attention and care to his wife. His wife Muthu wanted to live alone, since she was fed up with the shoddy treatment of her husband towards her. After three years of their separation, she died in an accident. Field Marshal Cariappa did not marry again and led a reclusive and lonely life, till his death. Gen. Thimmayya was a riddle and legend. He was the commander of the western command, at the time of partition and drove out the entire Pakistani tribal intruders from our Kashmir. He was confident of recapturing the western part of Kashmir, under occupation by Pakistan called Azad Kashmir, but Prime Minister Nehru did not allow him and went to the UN for a ceasefire. Due to difference of opinion with Defence Minister Krishna Menon, Thimmayya resigned from service in 1959, but the same was not accepted and he continued upto his retirement in 1961, just before the war with China. Since Gen. Thimmayya was a very able and powerful General, Krishna

Menon and Nehru were not on good terms with him. Both of them really feared an army take over by Gen. Thimmayya. We must give proper love and attention to our wives, otherwise there won't be any family life. Fidelity or faithfulness is an integral part of family life. If there is adultery and infidelity in married life, it is better to separate.' Devaiah made a lecture.

`My wife has no suspicion on me and I've not told her about my relation with doctor's wife. It is necessary to keep certain secrets in mind, otherwise family life will be in jeopardy' Chengappa expressed his opinion.

`In Islam, we are free to marry up to four wives. But, only a few people have more than one wife. If I divorced my wife by Triple Talaq, on some momentary impulse or anger, I can't take her back after change of mind. No purpose will be served with repentance. She has to marry another man and get divorce and that is called Nikah- Halala. Then only, I can take her back. The punishment for adultery in Islam is death by pelting stones. One of my relatives became angry against his wife since the biryani made by her was not tasty. After pronouncing Talaq, he became repentant since they had three beautiful daughters. When anger subsided, he was in tears, since she immediately left the house with children, to her father's house. His remorse and entreaties were of no avail. In Islam rules are rules and nobody can break it .Even wife can divorce her husband and that is called Khula. In mutual consent also we can separate and that is called Talaq-e-Mubarak' Rafeeque became eloquent.

`Rafeeque, some members of our community are of the view that Kodavas are not Hindus. We don't have the custom of tying mangalsutra or thali during marriages and no priest and dowry system. We give more importance to our ancestors and worship them as Gods and nature as Goddess. We also worship Kaveri Amma and other Hindu Gods, like Shiva, Vishnu, and Subramania etc. I strongly believe that this is one of the castes of Hinduism. The Lingayats also say that they have no connection with Hindu religion even though they worship all Hindu Gods. Lingayat Rajas were ruling us and our ancestors were soldiers under them. Our Hinduism is not a religion at all and it is a way of life. We are free to do anything. There are no rules to control a Hindu. We are free to believe in God. We are also free to live as atheist or agnostic. There is no compulsion that you should read Hindu mythology, Gita, Vedas, Upanishads etc and Hindus can live without reading anything related to their religion. I 'm free to go to the temple and nobody will ask me, if I did not go to the temple. We are answerable to God almighty and no one else. We can't see such a free religion, in the world, like Hinduism. Nowadays, our children do not try to understand what Hinduism really is. They don't have any time to read religious books and there is no school to educate them, about their religion. In Islam and Christianity, they can't escape from the study of their religions. I've seen children going to Madrasas for study of religion and in Christianity no boy or girl can marry without producing a certificate, showing that they have passed the examination in Bible studies .There is an organized set up there, but there is no such thing in Hinduism .' Chengappa made a long speech.

`Our Hindu Gods of mythology and Kings of Bharatvarsh had more than one wife. Now, we can't have more than one wife and so are Christians. We can divorce our wives, but that is denied to Christians. The only exception is Muslims. They can marry upto four and divorce without the help of court' Devaiah said.

`Dewan, don't discuss my affair with Nimmi. It'll reach the ear of Nina. If she knows anything about it, my life is gone and I'll be crucified by my wife'. Chengappa said.

`My dear Chengu, please believe me; I'll never share such things with anybody, especially my wife. She is a very innocent type woman but she can't hide anything in her mind. She will tell each and everybody with a preface: This is a big secret; please don't share it with anybody else.' Devaiah said in a humorous way.

`But, they will never share their secrets with anybody else, till their death.' Chengappa said

`Rafeeque, don't worry. We'll come to visit your estate at Kotagiri, shortly. We'll come one day with family but not for revelry, but for sightseeing.' Devaiah replied.

Dusk fell and the forest slowly plunged into darkness. The gentle contours of mountains could be discerned through the darkness. Tiny lights were twinkling at different parts of the mountains. It became noisy with the songs of lark and other nocturnal birds. The beetle and cricket also started singing and it seemed to be a whistling sound of high pitch .They saw many deer and rabbits, around them and their eyes shone like mirrors in the light of their torch, but they did not shoot any of them, for pastime. They talked for long four hours and returned home after 7.30pm. On the way, the forest people checked their jeep and one double barrel gun was recovered from the dick. They questioned them suspecting they were poachers.

`I'm Kodava and a retired army officer. I used to take my gun wherever I went' Devaiah replied boldly and they were let off without any further complications.

`Even now, they'll shudder at the mention of my father.' Rafeeque made a passing remark.

`I've heard about it. He was a terror when he was in service.' Chengappa said.

Rafeeque took his friends to their houses and returned home by 9pm. Jahanara was waiting patiently for him, at the door.

`Why are you so late? Did you catch any deer?'Jahanara asked.

`No Jahanara, the forest officials stopped our jeep on the way, checked it and recovered a double barrel gun from the dick. They questioned us for some time, under the impression we were poachers and released. They would have taken away the double barrel gun. Devaiah revealed his identity and then we were let off, immediately.' Rafeeque said.

`Our daughters've come in the evening. They've two days holiday at a stretch.'

`Where are they?'

`They've gone to sleep'.

`Dinner is ready. You look tired. Please come and have it '.

`I'll come after a thorough bath.'

`OK, hurry up. I want a rest since I've to get up early to prepare breakfast for our daughters '.

`Please wait for ten minutes.' Rafeeque rushed to the bathroom and Jahanara to the dining room.

@@@@@@@

4. Fire at Estate Factory Kotagiri

Next day, Jahanara got up from sleep at the crack of dawn and rushed to the kitchen. The maid Fatima was already at work when Jahanara entered the kitchen.

`Thatha sorry, I'm a bit late.' Jahanara said in an apologetic tone.

`Madam, why did you get up so early? I'll prepare everything. 'Fatima said humbly.

`Fatima, we've planned a trip to our estate at Kotagiri. You are also welcome. We can spend there two or three days and come back. This trip will help to get rid of the drudgery of life in an estate without seeing the world outside.' Jahanara said in excitement.

`I'm willing to come anywhere. What about Sultan and Beevi?' Fatima enquired.

`Rafeeque says somebody should be here. They don't feel boredom since they are couple. Let them stay in their quarters. We can close the house and go entrusting everything to Sultan and Beevi.'

After breakfast, they started the journey in their Innova car with Akbar Khan at the wheels. They chose the Muthumala route. The journey was dislocated at three places, due to the presence of herds of elephants, bison and bear on the road. At one place, a herd of bison and deer crossed the road in slow motion. By nightfall, they reached their estate. The manager Cherian was waiting for them. He had arranged food from a resort in the town. The weather was very chilly and the road was not visible due to thick fog. All of them were accommodated in the palatial estate bungalow which had five spacious bedrooms.

Next day, Rafeeque remained in the office and all others went out for sightseeing at Kotagiri and Coonoor locations. They were fully draped in sweaters and shawls and still they shivered. The entire hills and dales were in blazing colours. The roadside and hill tops were under the carpet of yellow. Small rivulets and brooks produced a melodious song .There was gaiety and joy everywhere. There was heavy rush of tourists in all places. They went through the Coimbatore highway for some distance and the view from there was glorious and marvellous. The estates looked like hanging gardens. There is a special odour and beauty for that landscape.

They spent full one day in the estate bungalow enjoying the biting cold and scenic beauty. Rafeeque discussed with Cherian and other Officers and arrived at a decision regarding the modernization of the factory. A firm in Bombay was contacted and work was assigned to them. He had lengthy discussions with the labour unions and agreed to enhance the bonus percentage. Many other benefits were also offered to the workers on condition that they will cooperate in giving more output.

That night at about 10pm, there was a fire in the factory. Rafeeque and family were viewing the TV when they heard a big explosion, rattling the windows and jarring some dishes from the table. When they looked out they saw an orange ball of flame rising to the sky. Rafeeque opened the door and rushed outside. He realized that the factory is on fire. He rushed to the spot and reached there within ten minutes. When he reached the location, he was panting excessively. He saw Cherian and other officers watching the fire from a distance and workers trying to put out the fire by pouring water. Before the fire tenders came, the fire was doused by the workers. The entire factory and the adjoining rooms were completely gutted. One hall was full of plucked leaves for processing. The adjacent room was main store and it contained full of processed tea, packing materials etc and everything became food for fire. A pall of thick black smoke hung over the entire area. Rafeeque and Jahanara were completely shattered in the loss of factory and stock of tea.

Next morning, Rafeeque sent his family to Kodagu and he remained in the estate. The following week, he was fully engaged with hectic activities. The manager had informed over phone all the concerned offices about the occurrence of fire in the factory. First came the Electrical Inspector and staff who made thorough investigation of the factory, the debris and ash to find out the cause of fire. They took some photographs of the site, collected some ash from the debris and examined the electrical guy wire. Then came police and they prepared an FIR and recorded statements of the company executives, workers and witnesses. They questioned the manager and trade union leaders to find out whether there were any labour problems in the estate. Thirdly came Revenue Officers, Village Officer and Tahsildar. Fourth visitors were Insurance company officers and they asked a number of questions to the manager, PRO and trade unionists. They took some photos of the site and collected some ash from the spot. Lastly came Plantation Inspector and Electricity Board officials.

After completion of everything, Manager Cherian came to Rafeeque and explained the details of total expenditure, in connection with the visit of the authorities.

`Sir, more than Rs 80,000/- was spent for the formalities'.

`OK, how much is expected as compensation from the government and Insurance Company.' Rafeeque asked Cherian.

`Sir, we can't predict anything now. Everything depends on the report of the Electrical Inspector. If he reports that the fire was due to short circuit, we are lucky. Since there is a labour dispute, the sabotage angle will be probed by police, even if we pay a lot of money for appeasing them. There is no guarantee that their report will be favourable to us. If the Electrical Inspector is sympathetic to us, he may write short circuit is the reason for fire. Then, the Insurance people can't reject the claim. Let us wait and see what happens.' Cherian explained.

`So the order placed on the Mumbai firm for renovation of the factory may be cancelled forthwith'. Rafeeque said.

` OK Sir, tomorrow itself they'll be addressed'. Cherian replied.

`We've to rebuild the factory and install new machinery, for which the compensation amount will be insufficient.'

`We can approach the government also for assistance, to install a new factory. This is a labour oriented industry and they can't ignore the people in this company. The Tahsildar has promised to help. ' Cherian said.

`For the time being, we've to find out another factory for processing our chap (leaf)'. Rafeeque said.

`We can give it to the Harrison company, Kotagiri '.

`We should acquire some more trucks for transportation of chaps'.

` OK, we can hire them on rent, locally.'

When Cherian left, Rafeeque went to the bedroom and stretched on the bed. He was tired mentally and physically. He slipped into a reverie. He saw his father clearly and he spoke to him with a sad and distraught face. He felt that he was crying and wiping the tears with a towel. After some time, he disappeared from sight and appeared again and continued his advice.

`Rafeeque, I'd done a lot criminal and sinful deeds in my life. I was complicit with Ponnappan in shooting hundreds of elephants and cutting thousands of sandalwood trees from the forest. Those who had associated with him in the criminal deeds are now millionaires and respected citizens of the country but Ponnappan is living as a fugitive somewhere, in the fear of death by state police or central forces. Some of his comrades were captured and they were awarded with death penalty for their illegal activities, but Ponnappan remained elusive from the hands of law. I didn't get peace of mind, till my death. Due to some kind of ego, I did not try to repent and seek redemption. I've amassed immense wealth for you, through illegal and Illegitimate means. You must be careful and cautious in your life to ward off the evil consequences of my deeds. Otherwise, the retribution will fall upon your head and those forces may even destroy your personal life. I'd been indecent and inhuman towards Revanna when he came and made a humble request. I did not show any sympathy or kindness towards him. He would have cursed me for my impolite, arrogant and inhuman behaviour. It remained a bleeding and festering wound in my mind, till my death. Once, I went to meet him in his house to beg pardon. By that time, he had given his daughter in marriage to an old widower. You should not be like your bapa, show love and kindness to others. Otherwise, you'll have to repent later.'

`Bapa, Bapa.....' Rafeeque got up from sleep and moaned.

Bapa had disappeared from his mind. Rafeeque lay in bed, for some more time and tried to recollect his words in the dream. He tried to scan the recent events in his life. He had cheated his wife several times in real life. He had his own explanation for such acts; that she was arrogant, aggressive and disrespectful towards him.

At this time, the faces of two ladies who had shared his bed, many years ago, appeared in the mirror of his mind. The first one was Sulekha, from Mananthavady. She was healthy, tall, fair, and chirpy and with a radiant face. She was the sister- in- law of the elder sister of his mother, Subaida. Sulekha was a young lady aged 35 years. Her husband was in gulf and used to come home, once in a year. Rafeeque and mother visited their house and stayed there, for two days when he was studying for Pre-University. Her husband's house was about 1 KM away from that house. She invited him to her house which is lying closed, after her husband returned to gulf. Now, her daughter is in college hostel at Calicut. She and her daughter had been living there alone for years. They used to go and clean up the house, occasionally. It was a backward area and people were very conservative and religious. Both of them went there in the evening and spent about two hours, there. On the way they met some neighbours and they looked at Rafeeque with distrust and prejudice. After entering the house, Sulekha closed the door and hugged Rafeeque and kissed him profusely. He was surprised at first and then he realized her intention. He responded favourably and they spent precious two hours in heaven. The neighbours who happened to see them while going to the house, spread the news and collected people to question them. After two hours, they heard a knock on the door. A lot of people had collected outside the house. They'd to face an irate mob and their entreaties fell on deaf ears. Rafeeque was caught, tied up to a tree in front of the house and his dress was examined for traces of semen. She was severely abused and a taunted. They had not experienced such a humiliation in their life. She began to cry and begged the mob to release him. They did not relent 'This youth is not your son or brother. You came here with evil and nefarious intention. This is equal to adultery and you deserve death by pelting stones according to Islamic law.' The people shouted. Then, she ran to the terrace of the two storeyed building and threatened with suicide. Finally, police arrived and they were rescued and taken to the police station. Seeing her relentless lament, the heart inside uniform melted and they were released unconditionally with a warning. No case was charged against them. It was really a nightmare and Rafeeque used to shudder, whenever he recalled that old incident. It was his first sex encounter in life.

Rafeeque recollected the meeting with Pramila, the wife of Excise Commissioner, in Room No. 212 of Paradise hotel, Kotagiri some years back. She was a proud lady with a sindur mark on the forehead. She spent hardly four hours with him, but that meeting had made an indelible mark on his mind. It was a rare experience and the sweet memories are still fresh in his mind. He tried to meet her again, but could not. She was a rare phenomenon. She was very healthy, active, cheerful, confident, bold and over sensuous, in temperament. He'd never experienced such ecstasy and pleasure from other ladies with whom he had slept.

She was brought to his room at 11Hrs by a hotel staff. There was a special charm and beauty to her face.

` Madam what is your name?' He shook hands with her and asked.

`Don't ask my name .Believe that I am Rekha 'She giggled.

`Where is your house?'

`Don't ask me such unnecessary and unpleasant questions. I came here to spend some blissful hours with you. Hurry up and send me back as early as possible.' She pleaded.

`How much will you get? I've paid a handsome amount to bring you here.'

`They may give me some three thousand and also meet the conveyance charge'. She said smilingly. When she smiled her face shone like a white dahlia blossom.

`Why are you in a hurry? '

`My children will return home from school, at 4.30pm and I should reach there before that.'

`Why are you cheating your husband? Is it for money or pleasure?'

`My husband is a big officer. He is getting too much money by way of salary, perks and bribe '

He pulled her towards him and whispered to her ear `then, why do you go out to meet other   people?'

`I want to teach him a lesson. He has many concubines. I suffered silently many years and then I became revengeful. They told me that you are the proprietor of a big tea estate and hence I came here. Money is not a problem for me. There is a big house and two cars in my residence. ' She made an enchanting smile and kissed him, caressed him and fell into the bed. She was just like an active volcano ready to erupt. The precious time spent with her is still fresh in his memory giving eternal pleasure and mirth to the mind.   When she left, Rafeeque felt an irreparable loss, agony and a ping in his heart. She was so sweet and charming in word and deed.

Rafeeque made enquiries about her with the hotel staff who brought her but he remained mute and silent. When enquired over and over again he opened his mouth.

`Her actual name is Pramila Devi. Her husband is Excise Commissioner. Further details I can't share with you. She is a rare visitor, even though she is in our client list. She agreed only after great persuasion. She will go out only once or twice in a year and that too if the party is a high profile VIP.' He replied with a smile.

Suddenly, a fear crept into his mind. If Jahanara came to know about his pleasure hunts, she may also become revengeful like Pramila Devi. He simply imagined his wife sleeping with another Person; then his face became grim and livid with anger

.A shudder passed through his spine and he said to himself ` I'll kill her if she showed any such acts of treachery and faithlessness'.

Rafeeque was held up at Kotagiri estate for about two weeks to settle various issues. The workers were very cooperative and the staff obedient. There was enough money in the bank to tide over the present crisis. If required, bank will give overdraft to make up the shortfall.

It was a chilly Friday and Rafeeque visited the nearby mosque and after namaz returned to the bungalow. Then, somebody came to the bungalow and rang the doorbell. Rafeeque went to the door and opened it. To his surprise, it was PRO and there was a lady along with him.

`Sir, I've brought a cook for you. You can have homely food.'

`OK, thank you. I'm fed up with hotel food '.

`Her name is Saira Bhanu and is living nearby. She will come in the morning and go home in the evening.' PRO Said.

`OK, thank you.'

PRO returned to his office within ten minutes.

Saira Bhanu covered her face with her shawl. Rafeeque showed her the kitchen and other parts of the bungalow. She spoke in Tamil and Hindi.

`Are you a resident of this place?'

`No sir, I'm from Calcutta. My husband is laid up. He was a supervisor in the Harrison Company.

We've spent a lot of money for his illness, still .there is no relief.'

`What is his name?'

`Freddy, he is an Anglo Indian. We've no connection with our families'

`Have you got any children?'

`Only one daughter and she is studying in 6th standard, in an English medium school'.

`Saira, don't cover your face with shawl. I'm Mohammed Rafeeque from Kodagu near Mysore'.

`OK Sir; after marrying Freddy, I'd done away with my burqa and started wearing churidar and sari. .At my home in Calcutta, all are using burqa with hijab.'

 When the veil was removed, he was surprised in the beauty and charm of that face. She had wheat complexion, chiselled features and had an angelic look. Her eyes were dreamy with a tinge of grief.

`My mother's ancestors were in Mysore' she said with some fear and trepidation.

`Mysore! Do you know the location?' Rafeeque enquired.

`I've only a faint memory. I've heard my mother say about him `He was a Sultan.'

`Tipu?'

` I think so.'

`What is the actual relation with Tipu Sultan?'

`He was my Ma's (mother) grandmother's grandfather'

`Tipu was lion of Mysore. He was Mysore Raja for some time. He was defeated by the British and his four wives and 16 children were exiled to Calcutta and the country handed over to the Wadiyars, the old rulers of Mysore. His tomb and garrison headquarters are still in Srirangapatna. My ancestors were soldiers in his army and they came from Kabul or Kandahar. Tipu's father Hyder Ali was a sepoy in the army of Nizam and later joined Mysore army. He was a brave and able soldier and rose in the army as a big commander, leading thousands of soldiers. The Mysore Raja was a weak monarch and it was easy for him to capture power, by dethroning the Raja. Hyder Ali's ancestors belonged to North West frontier province. He was also a Pathan and Khan. My father had told me the story of Hyder Ali and Tipu several times, when I was young. Tipu was an enigma and a tough ruler. He was a terror to the East India Company and for fighting with British he sought the help of France. It was he who brought the technology of rockets to India. So, for defeating him, the British sought the help of Nizam of Hyderabad and Marathas. It is heard that some of his commanders betrayed him and he was defeated and killed by British. He is held in high esteem by the Muslim community of Karnataka but other communities look at him with fear and hatred, since he had converted many Hindus and Christians into Islam .' Rafeeque narrated what he knew about the history of Tipu Sultan.

` But now, the relatives of Tipu are living in poverty and distress, in the City of joy.'

Saira Bhanu's face brightened for a moment and then became crestfallen.

`In Calcutta city, there is a big mosques dedicated to him. Tipu Sultan Shahi masjid at Dartamtalla Street, Calcutta, built by Prince Golam Mohammed, the grandson of Tipu Sultan. Now, hundreds of his relatives are living in that city. The glory, grandeur and pride of the successors of old monarch is not there. Still they have survived the onslaughts of time and fate. There were rivalries, fights and litigations among the relatives for property and wealth.

`In Karnataka, he is still considered as a powerful monarch and strict ruler. People remember him as erstwhile Mysore Raja. But, in other parts of South India, he is considered as a tyrant and religious bigot for the depredations done by him in Malabar and other parts of South India during his attack '.

`I don't know anything about him'

`Let us leave that subject .You can tell me your difficulties. I 'm willing to do any help for you.' Rafeeque assured her.

One day, Rafeeque enquired ` what is the illness of your husband?'

`He was a drunkard and spoiled his health. He is laid up for more than one year with liver cirrhosis. He took leave continuously for six months and finally he lost his job. Now, we are not getting any help from the company. We've to pay rent and meet other expenses. The income is zero and still we pull on. A lot of money is required for his medicines and other domestic needs. With the grace of Allah we are living.'

`I want to meet your husband. I would like to do some monetary help. Don't hesitate to tell me if you are in need of anything.'

Saira is an adept in cooking, mainly North Indian dishes. Rafeeque relished her food very much she came for work without any break and went home in the evening. He treated her with love and respect.

One morning, Rafeeque was sitting in the living room reading newspaper. Then, Saira came and made a request. `Sir, his condition has become worse. I've to take him to the Coimbatore Medical College. I want some money for meeting the expenses.'

`How much do you require?'

`One thousand rupees. Bulk of it will go for taxi. This may be recovered from my salary in Instalments.'

`Don't worry, I'll come with you. I'll come in the company vehicle and no need of engaging another conveyance.'

`It is very kind of you sir.' Saira Bhanu thanked him.

Next day at 7 am, Rafeeque went there in the company car driven by the company driver. It took some time to locate the house in the colony. It was a small house, in the middle of the cluster of houses, in an alley.

`Hallo Freddy, how are you? I'm Rafeeque proprietor of Livingston Estate' He introduced himself.

`Sir, thank you for your magnanimity.' Freddy said humbly.

`Who is your doctor at Coimbatore?'

`It is one Palaniswamy, Professor. He is MD, DM, and Gastro - Enterology Department. He is treating me for the last two years.' Freddy said.

` Did you stop liquor completely?'

`No sir, I've to take a small quantity of liquor, daily. Otherwise, withdrawal syndrome will cause more problems. Since I became an addict, I can't stop it.'

They went to the hospital directly and met the doctor at the appointed time. After thorough examinations and necessary investigations, the doctor told Rafeeque ` The condition of the patient is very serious. The only remedy is liver transplant and it will require 30 to 35 lakhs. To get liver under Cadaver scheme, you have to wait for at least two years.'

Rafeeque was sympathetic, but he could not afford such a huge amount, since he had a lot of urgent things to be done in his estate. They returned to Kotagiri in the evening, in a depressed state of mind. Rafeeque met all the expenses and paid an amount of Rs 3,000/- to Saira Bhanu to meet urgent requirements. She was very thankful to him and expressed it in a sob and smile.

Next day, she came in the morning and left home after preparation of the food.

`Saira, don't worry. If your presence is required at home, remain there. I'll arrange food from resort till your husband comes round to normalcy.' Rafeeque said.

`No sir, I'm witnessing this for the last many years. I'll come in the morning and return home after preparation of your food. I 'm too much indebted to you. I'll never shirk my responsibility. I've to show love and gratitude to my boss. Don't compel me to change my decision.' She pleaded.

`OK'

Freddy's condition continued serious for weeks. He felt difficulty to breath and fainted, occasionally. He was immediately admitted in a private hospital. He remained in coma for two days and breathed his last.

Rafeeque arranged everything in connection with his funeral of Freddy. Rafeeque and Cherian went to see the Vicar of the Catholic Church, there and arranged his funeral in the cemetery of their church, after necessary rituals and prayers. Saira Bhanu participated in the last rites. Nobody came from his house at Calcutta. All people related to Freddy and Saira were informed through Cherian and PRO. A function was conducted on the 41st day of the demise in the local church hall and all of them including Saira and all her neighbours in the colony participated.

`Cherian, I've some distant connection with her. Her ancestors and my ancestors came to India from the same place. My ancestors were in the army of Tipu and Wadiyar and she had some distant relation with the Sultan. So, it is my duty to help her in this time of distress. My wife may become angry, but there is no other go.' Rafeeque said.

Rafeeque took an independent house on rent, with spacious rooms and amenities and shifted her residence to that place. She continued her job in the estate as before. The new house was near the school of her daughter and for assistance and company an old lady was also engaged.

@@@@@@@

5. Rafeeque divorces Jahanara

The renovation work of the factory was commenced. The contract was given to a Mumbai firm for an amount of forty five lakhs. He took an overdraft of Rupees fifty lakhs from the bank for this purpose. After three months, Rafeeque made a visit to his house. Jahanara was in a happy and cheerful mood. She has managed the estates perfectly well in his absence. Akbar Khan was not only a driver, but he helped her in all fields. It was he who took the coffee to the curing company and acted as Liaison Officer in the sale of coffee to Nestle, Coffee board etc. Their daughters, Rabia and Zeenath are attending coaching classes for entrance examination, in an institute near their school. Rafeeque visited Kodagu in the weekend and met Chengappa and Devaiah and discussed various problems in their personal life and estates.

`Rafeeque, Devan is in a difficult situation now. His father had sold 250 acres to a lady doctor from Calicut. Now the Forest department says that the estate is in forest land. They had conducted survey on two occasions and fixed stone boundaries around the estate. Now, the doctor who is a retired professor, is running from pillar to post. The Forest department had given notice to her regarding take over and before they came to execute it, she approached High court and got a stay order. This is only a temporary relief and they'll have to conduct a protracted legal war with the department to get it back. Devan says that he is innocent in this case. For decades, this property was in their hands and they had paid land tax without fail.' Chengappa said.

`Sir, what about your son in US. When is his marriage going to be celebrated?'

`Rafeeque, we have to arrange his marriage. We've selected many girls who are from medical profession .One girl is a second year students of medicine at Bangalore. She belongs to a rich family, settled in Bangalore. Her father is a businessman on M.G.Road.

 We've selected half a dozen cases, from different parts of our state .He'll get only three weeks' leave. After his arrival here, he has to visit all the girls in a flash and select one girl and conduct the marriage without wasting time. There won't be time to celebrate the marriage. We can avoid all the functions and even engagement. He should get at least two weeks after marriage and hence only very few people can be invited for the marriage.' Chengappa explained.

`If you inform me in advance, I'll come and assist you'. Rafeeque said.

`Rafeeque, I want to select the girl. If I wait for him, everything will be in a mess.'

`Sir, it is not proper to select the girl by parents. Since he is in US, his mindset will be different and don't do anything like that without consulting him.'

`There'll be no engagement and pre -marriage functions. Then, he'll get some more days to spend here '.

`If there are Kodavas in US, why can't we select a girl from there?'

`Rafeeque, there are plenty of Kodavas settled in states but he is not interested in such girls. He wants a convent educated village girl who is well versed in Kodava cuisine, history and culture.' Chengappa said in one breath.

Rafeeque met Devaiah also. He was found in a depressed state of mind.

`Devaiah sir, you look worried; what is the problem?' Rafeeque enquired.

`Rafeeque, I'm passing through a difficult period. Hope everything will be OK soon.' Devaiah said.

`What is the problem that troubles you? Can I help you?' Rafeeque asked gently.

`Rafeeque, I've many problems. I don't think, you can help me in any way.'

`Treat me as a brother and tell me everything in detail.'

`My sons are running the estate. I've no role in the affairs of the estate. My wife is not well for quite a long time. She is completely laid up with rheumatoid arthritis. I've taken her to too many doctors at Bangalore and Coimbatore, but no relief. Hence, I brought a lady from Mysore to nurse her and for attending domestic chores. My sons do not like that lady since she is beautiful and young. They suspect that I've an affair with her and fear that quarter of the estate will go to her, if I marry her. They really fear that she'll claim some compensation, if she continues to serve for longer period. I want to conduct the marriage of my daughter, as early as possible. My sons have found out their mates from average families and they do not show any interest to find out a suitable groom for their sister. When I came to know about their selection, I raised some objections to their choice and this antagonised them and they started ill-treating me. Besides, there is also a property dispute. Father had sold some property to a lady doctor and now she has filed a case against me .The forest department says that, that property belonged to them .She says she was cheated by hiding the facts and want the transaction cancelled and the amount refunded. Father sold this property for the marriage of my two sisters. Can you find out a solution for these vexing problems?' Devaiah said in distress.

`Don't worry, we can find out an amicable solution for all the annoying problems. Let me think over it and I'll let you know my suggestions, to tide over the present crisis. Nothing can be gained, by worrying unnecessarily.' Rafeeque tried to console him.

Rafeeque returned to his house and discussed with Jahanara the problems of Devaiah and she readily found out a solution, within minutes According to her, the first priority is the marriage of his daughter. If anything happens to his wife, his daughter will be in anguish and misery. Regarding the maid, she suggested not to keep a maid for more than two years. Send her home with a handsome amount as gift or reward for her service and find out another lady. As regards the case, filed by the lady doctor, let the litigation with the forest dept. come to an end and then it can be sorted out. Give a suitable affidavit in the court that the party who sold the property is not alive and the present owner has no hand in this sale and proceed with the civil case to its final verdict. Tell him not to worry, unnecessarily.

Rafeeque was stunned in the practical wisdom of his wife. He conveyed his suggestions to Devaiah, immediately and he did as was advised by Rafeeque .Within one month, a groom was found out for Preethy, the daughter of Devaiah and marriage arranged in a modest way. Rafeeque and Jahanara participated in the marriage. In the auditorium, he was embarrassed on seeing his old sweetheart Krithika on the stage with the groom; but escaped from the venue without giving a chance to see eye to eye with her.

`Let us go home. I've to return to Kotagiri today itself.' Rafeeque prompted and prodded Jahanara, when the marriage function was going on.

`Marriage is going on and how can we return without meeting the couple? Also, it is not correct to skip the lunch?' Jahanara remarked.

`I've met Devaiah sir, blessed his daughter and informed him that I would return home immediately, after the marriage.' Rafeeque said in a faint worried tone.

` What has happened to you? Are you afraid of anybody? Why are you perspiring?' Jehanara said.

Rafeeque again prodded and nudged Jahanara and left the auditorium without participating in the feast.

After reaching Kotagiri, Rafeeque spoke to Devaiah over phone and enquired 'Who is your son- in- law and what is he? What is his connection with Krithika who was my class mate? '

'He is a junior advocate in our Bar. He is the son of Krithika .His brothers are high officers in Defense .It is a good alliance. I'm very much satisfied and relieved now. If anything happens to my wife, there is nothing to worry. My daughter is in safe hands.'

Within one year, the son of Chengappa arrived and married a lovely medical student hailing from a rich family of Bangalore. Rafeeque and Jehanara participated in this marriage also. The bride is a lovely girl studying for third year MBBS, in Jain College.

The renovation work of the factory was awarded to a Mumbai firm and they commenced the work. In this connection, he took an overdraft of Rupees fifty lakhs from the bank. The insurance case came to an end and they passed an order for payment of a compensation of Rupees twenty five lakhs. It was a big relief for Rafeeque, even though he had to give a fees of five lakhs to the advocate.

Rafeeque purchased the rented house of Saira Bhanu for 18 lakhs and Rupees one lakh was deposited in her bank account, to make her life safe and secure. She and her daughter thanked him for his benevolence and generosity. This charity shown to Saira Bhanu had its after-effects also. There was a gossip in the estate circles that Rafeeque has married Saira Bhanu and they are living as man and wife.

One day, Jahanara's brothers Jaleel and Nazar paid a visit to the estate, on their way to Coimbatore. At that time, Rafeeque had gone to the house of Saira Bhanu, for arranging a renovation work to the house. Somebody told them that he was living with the maid, after her husband's demise. They also told them about his occasional revelries in Paradise hotel. They were shocked and their mind simmered with anger and vengeance. They collected the details of the lady and the location of the house and wanted to visit the house to verify the truth. They made a surprise visit to the house and then Rafeeque and Saira were inside. They knocked on the door and after ten minutes the door was opened by Saira Bhanu.

`Who are you? What do you want?'

`We want to meet Rafeeque.' Jaleel said.

Then she called Rafeeque ` Rafeeque sir, somebody has come to meet you.'

After five minutes, he came to the door and faced his brothers-in-law.

 On seeing them, Rafeeque was shocked and taken aback.

`We are on our way to Coimbatore. We had gone to the estate and some of the workers told us that you are staying here and hence we came here to see your new house.' Jaleel said.

Rafeeque was terribly embarrassed in the sudden fright and his face became blushed and contorted.

`What do you want? I came here just now. This is the house of my maid. There is some maintenance work here and I came here to supervise the work. I'll go back now itself. Come with me to the bungalow.'

`Somebody of your staff told me that you are staying here. We've to go to Coimbatore and return home today itself.'

`Why didn't you inform me earlier? I would've arranged your lunch?' Rafeeque babbled incoherently. His face became distorted and convulsed in fright.

`OK, Rafeeque, we are leaving.' Jaleel replied.

Jaleel and Nazar were fully convinced that she was his second wife. They returned to Virajpet after cancelling their Coimbatore trip. On hearing this news, Jahanara became aggrieved and cried like a child, in the treachery of her husband. They made some secret plans to counter the infidelity and deception of Rafeeque. Brothers advised Jahanara to demand a power of attorney for the two estates which she was managing. It'll be a great support for her and family and can transfer the ownership to her name or to the name of her daughters. They met a document writer and prepared a power of attorney and awaited the arrival of Rafeeque.

After two weeks, Rafeeque made a visit to his house and then she informed her brothers to come to Virajpet, immediately. Jahanara never showed any sign of her knowledge of his treachery. Her brothers visited the house along with their goons.

`Rafeeque Bhai, we have come to know that you've another wife and many concubines at Kotagiri. It is your freedom and we don't interfere in that. But, for the security of our sister and her daughters we want you to transfer these two estates to her name, immediately. The document will be written today itself and the registration can be done, tomorrow.'

`It is my father's property. How can I transfer that to her name? I'll never do that, even if you kill me.'

`OK, if you are against it; then write a power of attorney. She is managing these estates and this document is highly necessary, for running the estates.'

`No, I can't do it '

`Then, we'll have to use force. My sister and children will suffer if you continue like this. You are Spending lakhs for your concubines. You spent about 20 lakhs for your maid. Is it true? I've all facts and figures with me and don't compel us for more drastic measures.' Jaleel said in anger and indignation

Finally, Rafeeque expressed willingness to give a power of attorney to his wife Jahanara on condition, that it 'll never be misused. Immediately, they went out and returned with a document writer and District Registrar. Within a short time, the document was prepared and handed over to Jahanara. After that, all of them left the house.

In the evening Jahanara and Rafeeque had a quarrel.

`What is the name of your new wife?' Jahanara asked angrily.

`I've got only one wife and that is Jahanara.' Rafeeque said emphatically.

`Then, who is this Saira Bhanu?'

` She is only my maid '

`People say you are living with her. Have you married her?'

`No, it is not correct. It is true that I've done some humanitarian help to that lady since she had nobody there, after the demise of her husband. '

` My brothers have collected full details regarding Saira and other concubines. It is open secret at Kotagiri.'

` It is a lie. Somebody with ulterior motive has tried to break my family.' Rafeeque said in dismay.

`There won't be smoke without fire 'Jahanara retorted.

`Jahanara, believe me. I've no connection with that lady. It is nothing but jealousy of a section of my staff.'

`How much did you spend for her house? People say that you are living with her. How can I disbelieve them?'

`Jahanara, why do you blame me, unnecessarily?'

`You may say that you can have up to four wives. But, I can't tolerate that. If you want to live with her I don't stop it. You live with her. If you want to spend thousands for concubines, you can do it, but you can't expect me to share your bed, again. You are free to do anything you like. But, leave us free. Let us live anywhere peacefully.' Jahanara blurted out in anguish and grief.

Rafeeque approached Jahanara and tried to touch her chin.

`Darling, my dear '

`Don't touch me. I trusted you blindly and you cheated me. I can't live with such a man like you.'

`You and your brothers are my enemies. If they think they have won, they are mistaken. For the future of my family, I agreed to their demands. Your brothers and their goons have coerced me to write the Power of attorney. But, I would like to tell you that I can cancel or modify that document at any time 'Rafeeque shouted at Jahanara.

`If I don't have such a document with me, what is the guarantee that you'll not bring your second wife to this house?'

`Never, it is only the figment of your imagination'.

`You are a cheat, womanizer and rake '.

`Shut up, you slut, harlot and whore. Don't try to fight with me. If I want, I can pack you up any moment. If you are from Babur's land, I'm a Pathan and my ancestors came from the same place. I've also the same mental calibre as your people'

Rafeeque became infuriated and slapped on her face, twice. She shrieked loudly and the maids came rushing to save her.

`Go to the kitchen all of you and don't try to pamper this slut.' Rafeeque shouted.

 Hearing the orders of Rafeeque, the maids became scared and withdrew to the kitchen.

`If you don't love and respect me, I don't want such an arrogant wife. Talaq, Talaq, Talaq.' Rafeeque fumed and thundered.

`You are a debeaucher and rapist and still you have divorced me. I'll kill you and then I'll commit suicide.' She cried in anger and mental agony.

She took the flower vase from the table and struck him on his shoulder. Jahanara was fuming with rage. Rafeeque then ran inside and returned with a knife and stabbed her in the stomach.

Jahanara made a loud scream, shuddered with pain and fell down. Blood flowed profusely from the wound. The maids and driver came out and tried to stop the blood by a cloth. Rafeeque was frightened and he ran out, started the car and fled.

Jahanara began to cry loudly.

`He has killed me. He is a rogue and butcher. Oh! Allah save my life. He is a vampire and he wants to suck my blood. Take me to the hospital or I'll die.' She lamented.

Then, all the maids and driver rushed to the porch, carried her to the jeep and sped to the hospital. The doctors examined her and she was immediately subjected to an urgent operation.

Jahanara lay in the hospital for about 14 days. On the second day of the admission, the local Inspector of Police visited the hospital and enquired about the incident and prepared an FIR. Jahanara was in a dazed mood and she could not reply properly to the questions .He told her that he would visit the house after her discharge from hospital. Beevi and Sultan were with her always till discharge. Jahanara's brothers Jaleel and Nazar visited her in the hospital and offered all help to teach that bastard a lesson.

`We are prepared to avenge the attack 'They said.

`Bhayya, don't do that. Afterall, he is the daddy of my daughters. Allah will give him the deserving punishment for his misdeeds. Let us not take revenge on him now.' Jahanara entreated.

`Tell us if you require any kind of help, money or goons?'

`Bhayya, let us be patient and punish him through the criminal case charged by police.'

`OK, we respect your sentiments. We can meet a good criminal advocate and see that he is punished'Jaleel said in indignation.

` My life is ruined.' Jahanara sobbed.

`Even if he comes for reconciliation, he can't live with you.'

`Is it so? You have to marry another person and get divorce, for reunion with him.'

`That is impossible '

`Don't worry about it. You think about your children. Let him go to hell.' Nazer said. Jahanara did not inform her daughters about the attack. She spent two weeks in the hospital and then got discharged. Her urinary bladder, uterus and intestine had been damaged in the attack .There was too much loss of blood and required transfusion of four bottles of blood . After two weeks Jahanara came round to normalcy and got discharged from the hospital.

Rafeeque went to the house of Saira Bhanu. He was received by her warmly and gave him tea and eatables. He was in a state of shock and fear.

`Saira, I don't want anything now. I don't feel any appetite.'

`Are you coming from Kodagu?'

`Yes, I'm coming after a big fight with my wife, Jahanara. In a fit of anger, I stabbed her. I 'm afraid whether she has survived the attack or not. Police may come any time. I want to hide somewhere'.

 Saira Bhanu was terrified on hearing the story. Her mind was filled with anxiety and fear.

`Sir, don't go to your estate now. Go and hide somewhere or meet an advocate and seek his advice. Don't worry about us. My daughter and I'll live somewhere. I'm very much worried and aggrieved.' She lamented.

`Saira, I can't go back to my house. I've slapped Triple Talaq on Jahanara. Now, I'm afraid to go anywhere. If you don't show sympathy towards me, I'll go somewhere and finish my life.' Rafeeque warned and threatened Saira Bhanu.

Saira began to weep and she was consoled by Rafeeque `don't worry, I'll look after you.'

Rafeeque went to the mosque, prayed, met the muezzin and came back with a Maulvi. Rafeeque opened his mind to the Maulvi and sought his advice.

`Son, don't worry .We should not lose heart in the event of bad luck or unpleasant happenings. We must keep our cool and think over it wisely. There'll be a solution for all intricate problems.'

Rafeeque called Saira Bhanu to his side and whispered. ` Allow him to conduct our Nikah now'.

Saira was terrified and refused his request outright.

`Be calm and cool. Now you are in danger. Try to save yourself. I can't agree to any Nikah now. My daughter will never agree for that. Leave me alone. Let us live anywhere in poverty and misery. I don't want the help of anybody.' Saira Bhanu blurted out in anger.

Rafeeque did not relish her talk and his face became sad and crestfallen.

`If you don't like me, I'll go anywhere and finish my life. I love you so much and if you also hate me, I've no option before me other than suicide.' Rafeeque threatened.

Saira Bhanu looked like an insane woman; she rushed to him, hugged him and cried profusely.The Maulvi was perplexed and embarrassed on seeing the poignant scene.

`Maulvi, please recite some verses from the holy Quran to drive away evil spirits and gins so that there'll be lasting peace in this house.' Rafeeque entreated.

 As requested by Rafeeque, Maulvi sat down, closed his eyes and began to recite some Quran verses from memory and then stood up and placed his palm on the head of Rafeeque and Saira Bhanu. Then, he went to the four corners of the house and repeated the verses.

He came inside and told Rafeeque `Son, your time is very bad. Have you broken your namaz? Pray to Allah and only he can save you from the dangers.'

Rafeeque embraced the Maulvi, paid him a handsome amount and took him back to his house in his car. After returning from outside, he sat in a pensive mood for some time. Saira Bhanu gave him breakfast but he refused. He rose from his seat, went to a room and fell to the bed and went to deep slumber with anxiety and tension.

Rafeeque stayed in that house for two days without informing anybody in the estate .He feared that police will come to arrest him. He was in great anxiety and fear whether Jahanara has survived the attack. He dialled the house of the supervisor Govindaswamy and enquired about Jahanara. He informed him that she was admitted to the hospital and she was out of danger. Then, Rafeeque heaved a sigh of relief and made a vow to visit Ajmer- Dargah later, for saving the life of Jahanara.

@@@@@@@

6. Rafeeque convicted for 5 years

Rafeeque informed his friends Chengappa and Devaiah about the unhappy incident with Jahanara and sought their help to settle the issue. Both of them met Jahanara in the hospital and made enquiries about the quarrel. They advised her not to precipitate the issue and try for an early amicable settlement.

`The police have registered a criminal case against the murder attempt. He don't want his wife and children. He has another wife at Kotagiri and many concubines. Then, how can I agree for a negotiated settlement? He has also slapped triple talaq on my head.' Jahanara said in anguish.

`Be careful while giving statement to the police. A slip of tongue will land him in prison.' Chengappa said.

`Sir, I'll be careful. But, how can I show sympathy on a person who slapped triple talaq on me?' Jahanara replied in anger.

`Jahanara, be patient. After all, he is your husband.' Chengappa again said.

`Sir, he is no longer my husband. He has snapped our ties with a simple quarrel. He'll never come to my life, again. My life is ruined'. Jahanara began to sob.

`We hope everything will become normal with the passage of time, as before'. Devaiah tried to console her.

Chengappa and Devaiah returned home after spending there, about 30 minutes. They helped Rafeeque to get advance bail through Ashik, but it did not succeed. Hence, as advised by

Ashik, Rafeeque came to Virajpet, surrendered in the court and got bail.

After discharge from hospital, Jahanara was relaxing in her room when she heard the ring of doorbell. On opening the door, they were surprised to see the Police Inspector and another policeman standing at the door. They were invited inside and offered seats in the drawing room and Jahanara sat opposite to them. They asked a lot of questions and Jahanara replied to all of them with clear cut answers.

`What is your name?' The Inspector asked.

`Jahanara.'

`Age?'

`37'

`What is the name of your husband?'

`Mohammed Rafeeque.'

`How old is he?'

`He is aged 45'

`Why did he stab you and at what time?'

`He is living at Kotagiri, Ooty and looking after our tea estate, there. That day, he came to our house in an angry mood and quarrelled with me, without any provocation from my side. In a fit of anger he abused me and my brothers and slapped on my face. Also, he slapped triple talaq on my head. Out of grief and distress, I shouted back at him and tried to hit him with a flower vase. It did not cause any injury to him. Then, he became violent, went inside, came out with a knife and stabbed me in the stomach and ran away. This occurred at 4-30 pm on Friday the 11th' instant.

`What is the provocation for the quarrel?'

`At Kotagiri, he is having another wife. My brothers happened to hear about this when they visited the estate, on their way to Coimbatore. He recently purchased a house to this lady for Rupees eighteen lakhs. Hence, my brothers insisted him to prepare a power of attorney to me, for running these two estates, here. He is a spendthrift and for the security of our daughters and me, we demanded that and he readily agreed for the same. After my brothers left, he became angry and quarrelled with me. When I questioned his treachery and splurge, he lost his temper and slapped on my cheeks, slapped triple talaq on my head and stabbed me in the stomach with a knife.'

`Is that knife available here?'

`No, he has taken it with him when he left after the incident.'

`At the time of the incident, what was your dress?'

`I wore churidar and shawl and there was no headscarf. That dress was completely drenched in blood.'

`Is that dress available here?'

`Yes, it is here'.

Jahanara went inside and brought the blood stained churidar and handed over the same to   the police. The Inspector called the kitchen staff and asked ` do you know who stabbed Jahanara madam?'

`It was done by Rafeeque sir' Beevi and Fatima said in unison..

`Did you see it with your own eyes?'

`No sir, we heard a shriek from madam and came out to see what happened. Madam was crying aloud and he slapped her in our presence. Then, he shouted at us and asked us to go back to kitchen. We heard a scream after a few minutes and when we came out she was lying on the floor in a pool of blood and blood was oozing from the wound. We tried to stop the bleeding with cloths but failed. Rafeeque Sir was standing in a menacing mood with a knife. He stood there for a few seconds and then went out, started the car and left.' They said in unison. `

 After the domestic maids, the driver Akbar Khan also was questioned by the police. It took one hour for recording their statements and they left the premises with an advice. ` You'll be called to the court and then you should not deviate from the statement given to us now. If you want you'll get a copy of the statements from the office.'

`OK Sir, we'll be careful to give the same reply, in the court also.' Jahanara said.

When they were about to leave, Jahanara called the policeman and handed him a cover.

After six months, they got summons from the court and all of them went there and deposed before the magistrate. They had engaged an advocate named Rama Rao, in addition to the public prosecutor. The counsel for Rafeeque was one Manjunath. He was really a terror. He resorted to many threats and shouting to harass Jahanara and other witnesses when they were cross examined by him, but they were firm and resolute in their reply.

Adv. Manjunath asked many confusing and perplexing questions to Jahanara and she replied to them with clear and specific replies. Finally he asked ` do you know the man standing in the box?'

`Yes, he is my old husband'.

`That means he is nobody to you now.'

`Yes, he was my husband but not now. He has slapped triple talaq on my head and he has ceased to be my husband from that moment.'

`Is he the father of your children?'

`Yes, he is the father of my children.' Jahanara admitted.

`Then, it is your bounden duty to save him from conviction.'

`If he has done criminal offence, he should suffer the punishment for the same.'

`As a legally married wife, it is the duty of the wife to save the husband from conviction. Why are you reluctant to do that?' The advocate shouted.

`Since he has divorced me by triple talaq, I've no moral responsibility to save him from conviction, even if he is the father of my two daughters. If he has done anything heinous and unbecoming of a husband he should get the punishment for the same.' Jahanara said boldly.

Many people including his friends Chengappa, Devaiah, estate supervisors and Planters Association President had come and requested Jahanara to be precise in reply with a view to save him from conviction. But, Jahanara stood firm like a rock and thus her deposition in the court led to the conviction of Rafeeque.

The case proceeded for over one year. Finally, Rafeeque was convicted for simple imprisonment for 5 years. The appeals given in the higher courts were rejected and thus after two years he went to Parappana Agrahara jail .Before going to jail, Rafeeque made many attempts to marry Saira Bhanu, but she refused on the ground that her daughter was against such a marriage. She was very sympathetic towards him, but she never succumbed to his passions and desires. Rafeeque lived in one room and Saira and her daughter slept in the other room. He appointed Saira Bhanu, as store keeper in the estate factory. Full authority was given to the Manager Cherian and PRO Ramaswamy to run the estate in his absence.

In the jail, life was simple and peaceful. For killing time, he resorted to reading books of all genres. He read holy Quran several times and tried to understand the rules to live as a true Muslim. Also, he read Bible and Hindu mythology. Then, he took to world classics, American literature and also Kannada literature. He had a passion for the works of Leon Uris and read with passion his two novels available in the library- Exodus and Redemption. He read the novels of Arthur Hailey such as Airport, Hotel, Final Diagnosis, Money Changers etc. His reading habit has transformed his life, completely. He found out the writings of Sri. M very fascinating. He liked and enjoyed very much the Himalayan adventures of Sri .M, his novels and his writings on Vedas and Upanishads etc. Later he found out that Sri. M was also a Pathan like him. He found out that his real name was Mumtaz Ali. He and his parents were living in Trivandrum and later moved to Chennai. He was wandering during his school and college days in search of eternal peace and knowledge. He is now a spiritual guru of both Muslims and Hindus and presently engaged in social work and education of downtrodden people, in a remote village in Andhra. He read all the books available in the jail library. He occasionally recalled his precious two days with his classmate, Krithika. He thought ` My son Ashik is living as a Hindu and this secret will remain forever in my mind, till my death. Devaiah's daughter is my daughter- in- law. My son will become a big advocate and later a judge.'

In the cell, he had two companions as inmates, namely Abdul Sathar and Jos Antony from Bangalore. Abdul Sathar belonged to a rich family of Hebbal. He was undergoing life imprisonment for murder. He lent a huge sum of money to one of his close friends named Anwar without any documentary proof. He was a film Director and wanted to produce a new film in Kannada. A story was selected, a script was prepared and some actors were chosen, but, even after two years, the shooting of the film was not started. His friend did not return the money despite many reminders. One day, he had a quarrel with his friend and it ended in the murder of Anwar. Sathar was arrested and tried and convicted for life. They had two school going children. Sathar has already completed 3 years in jail .His wife is in perpetual agony and grief and visits the jail once in two weeks.

The second inmate Jos Antony was convicted for causing grievous injury to a man suspected to be the paramour of his wife Lucy. Antony was running a grocery store, at Jalahalli. He was in Air Force and retired after 15 years of service. They had no children even after five years of marriage. He and his wife had undergone all types of treatment but in vain. They were living peacefully in their own house near the church. One day, Antony visited his house at about 11am. He saw a strange footwear outside the house. He became suspicious and closed the main door from outside and went to the rear door with an iron rod and knocked. He waited there for ten minutes and finally the door was opened by Lucy. She was trembling with fear. When Jos Antony went inside, a middle aged man was found hiding inside. He struck him on his head with the iron road and the stranger fell down unconscious. Antony and Lucy took this fellow to the nearby hospital. He was under treatment in the hospital for about one month and eventually discharged as a cripple. Right side of his body was completely paralysed. His wife lodged a complaint with the police and they registered a case and arrested Antony. The injured person, Thomas was an employee of a supermarket and was residing in the vicinity of Antony's house. Antony confessed to the court about the incident and he was convicted for 5 years of simple imprisonment. Antony is always in a moody and reclusive mood. He used to talk to others very rarely. He is harbouring a guilty conscience that he had ruined a family. Thomas can hardly walk with crutches inside the house but he is unable to go to work. He is not getting any salary after the accident. He has to spend a lot of money for medicine and physiotherapy. His wife is now working as maid in the neighbouring houses to make money for livelihood and treatment of her husband. They have three school going children. After the conviction of Antony, his wife went to the house of her brother.

Rafeeque did not expect any visitor in jail .But after three months, his Manager and PRO visited him in jail and discussed various issues connected with the estate .They had brought a letter from Saira Bhanu. He was very much delighted on receipt of the letter. She had written that she was unable to travel, all the way to Bangalore to meet him and prayed for his health and happiness. After a period of six months, on a bright Friday, he was surprised on seeing his friends Chengappa and Devaiah at the reception counter. After Friday prayers, he was relaxing in the cell when he was informed that some visitors had come to meet him. He was overexcited and overjoyed in meeting them, after many months.

They talked till the end of the stipulated time and parted, promising another visit, after six months. He expected that his daughters will visit him, but nothing happened.

`Devan sir, how is your wife now?' Rafeeque enquired.

`Rafeeque, her condition is very bad. She was in Manipal hospital, for about one month. She is now completely bedridden. I've sent back the old maid and brought a new one named Maya, from Mysore. She is a distant relative of my wife and is a widow above 35 years, with a son aged 10 years. I brought the boy also with her. Now, that house is noisy with the music and shouting of that little boy. My wife thanked me for doing such charitable activities. But, my sons detest her and her son. What to do? They are over selfish. They do not agree for marriage also. They suspect that I 'm too much attached to that lady and may marry her, if anything happens to their mother. Money cannot solve such problems. The new lady was very loving and hard working. She was almost like a sister to my wife. All the domestic chores and nursing will be done by her. As requested by my wife, I admitted the boy in an English medium school, near my house, in 4th standard 'Devaiah elaborated.

Chengappa did not have anything to say and he stood silent hearing the story of Devaiah.

`Chengappa sir, how is your daughter- in- law. 'Rafeeque enquired.

`She is in the final year. My son has no idea to take her for two years. He had spoken to me that she has to complete her course, house surgeoncy etc. and then only she would be taken to US.'

`So, it'll take two years, minimum.' Rafeeque said.

`Yes, I think so.'

They spoke about various subjects, till the allotted time was over. When they left the jail, Rafeeque returned to his cell in distress and mental agony.

After a couple of days, Rafeeque had another visitor. He was surprised to see that his sweetheart Saira Bhanu and her daughter were waiting to see him. He was overjoyed and his eyes became wet with ecstasy and delight.

`Rafeeque sir, sorry for not coming earlier. Now she has got two days holiday at a stretch and decided to visit you. We started in the early morning and should reach home before night fall'

`Thank you very much for taking pain to travel all the way from Kotagiri to Bangalore, by bus.'

`We had a difficult time to find out the jail after reaching Bangalore.' Saira Bhanu said.

`Namaste sir, how are you?' Jessinda wished him with folded hands.

`Beti, thank you for your love 'Rafeeque said.

`You had this fate because of me. We are very much indebted to you. If you had not come for our rescue, what would have been our plight now? No doubt, the society would have dubbed me a prostitute. Most of the destitute ladies end up in brothels. How can I repay the debt?' Saira became sad and sentimental and she began to weep.

`Saira don't cry. Our fate is predetermined. It is not because of you. At the time of my birth, my destiny was written by Allah. You have nothing to do with that.' Rafeeque became philosophical.

`We are very much aggrieved in your conviction and jail life. What can we do for you?'

`You have not done anything wrong to me. I've great respect towards you because you are really a bold lady. I'm meeting such a lady like you, for the first time in my life. Ordinary ladies lack such will power, grit and determination. They are like creepers and will climb over any tree, shrub or wall .You are not like that. You are pure and your character is stainless. When I was sleeping in the cell on the first day, I realized the greatness of your character. You are unblemished and pure as lily. I tried to make you my own and failed this is not praise or eulogy, but real appreciation of your character. You should live for your daughter. I'll do all help as your employer.' Both the eyes of Rafeeque became watery again.

`Beti, how is your studies?'

`Uncle, going on smoothly. I've got first in the last examinations.'

`Good, congratulations.'

`Thank you, uncle.' Jessinda said in delight.

They returned to Kotagiri, immediately after the meeting. Saira Bhanu was sobbing when she turned to go back. Her mind was tormented by grief and agony.

@@@@@@@

7. Jahanara's agony and ecstasy

Jahanara tried to forget the past as a nightmare. She tried to wipe out the memory of Rafeeque, from her mind. Anger and revenge surged in her mind but she had no chance to settle scores with her old husband. By that time, he had gone to jail. When her daughters came home after their +2 examinations, she tried to apprise them in brief about the unhappy incident which took place at their house, in their absence.

` Your daddy is a debaucher and cheat. He has another wife and many concubines, at Kotagiri.

He recently purchased a house for his new wife for an amount of eighteen lakhs. He'll give his estate also for these whores and harlots. When I mentioned about this, he slapped me and stabbed me in the stomach. I was immediately taken to the hospital, subjected to immediate operation and was in the hospital for two weeks. For the cruelty and infidelity to his legal wife, he got the deserving punishment. He is now in Parappana Agrahara jail.' Jahanara narrated the incident.

The girls were in tears. They wept silently in the misfortune of the family.

`Mummy, we want to meet our daddy.'

`Don't think about daddy. He hates all of us and then why do you worry about him?'

`We can't believe it. He is not such a rogue. He is a loving person. What happened to him in such a short time?' Both of them lamented in unison.

`He slapped triple talaq on my head 'Jahanara said in grief.

`Mummy, what is it?'

`He has divorced me .He is no longer my husband.'

` For reunion with him what should we do?'

`It is impossible. A reunion is out of question. To reunite with him, I've to marry another person and then get divorce'.

`It is a wretched thing. How can you marry another man and get divorce. We don't want such a reunion. Let him go his own way. Why did he behave in such a thoughtless way?'

`He has a wife and family there. We are unwanted people.'

Jahanara began to sob and her daughters joined her in her anguish and grief.

Rabia and Zeenath spent the holidays silently in their house. One day, they went to Bangalore for writing the entrance examination. After one month, the +2 result came and both of them were placed in first class. But, in the entrance test their rank was far behind and did not get selection, in government quota, for medicine. Jahanara met Chengappa and he through a friend arranged two seats, in the Christian Medical college, Bangalore. A huge amount was required in connection with donation, admission charges and other fees.

The Bank Manager came to their rescue and he sanctioned two education loans for the girls. For this purpose, Jahanara visited Bangalore many times, in their jeep with driver Akbar Khan.

The driver Akbar Khan was the son of a distant relative of her father. He was like a family member in that house. He belonged to a poor family of Gundlupet. He had to look after his old parents and two grown up sisters. Jahanara was very considerate towards him and helped him financially on many occasions. He was very faithful in all respects. He used to take her to the Hassan estate frequently and return home very late in the night. He took her to the Coffee Board office, Spices Board office, the planter's union office, coffee curing mill, coffee trader's office, Banks etc.

Jahanara entrusted money matters and disbursement of salary of workers etc. to Akbar Khan. One day, they went to Hassan estate in the evening. Since there was some work in the estate and disbursement of salary to the workers, the return journey was delayed, inordinately. At 10.30 pm, they finished everything and boarded the jeep. On the way, they were stranded near bell -mouth of main road, in the dead of the night. There was a roadblock on the way, due to falling of a big tree across the metalled road leading to her estate. They could not go back to the estate, since the road was narrow and sloppy. In the front light of the vehicle, Akbar tried to reverse the vehicle, but failed. There was no human habitation in that area and no glimmer of light, anywhere. They were stranded on the road, the whole night. There was pitch darkness in the road and occasional sounds of wild animals. Leaving the vehicle, they walked back to the estate, slowly. There was no houses nearby and they did not see any streak of light. They were terrified by the howling and roar of wild animals. They heard trumpeting of an elephant closeby. One wild boar came and sniffed at Jahanara's dress with its snout and ran away. They heard the sound of a wolf and fox at close quarters. Jahanara shuddered with fright. She spread her shawl under a tree and sat down, with anxiety and fear. She tried to stretch and relax her body on the bed of dried leaves under the tree.

`Akbar, I'm afraid and shivering with cold; please give me a blanket '. Jahanara pleaded in the darkness

`Madam, it is not safe to sit here. The elephant may come here any time and we have no shelter here to escape. Better we can go back to our jeep and spend the night there.'

`Then, we can go back. Please help me to stand up.' Jahanara requested.

Akbar Khan gripped her hand tightly and helped her to stand erect. She was still shivering. They slowly walked back to the jeep and she got inside. Akbar covered her properly with the shawl and still she was feeling chilly and uncomfortable. Akbar fished out another woollen sheet from the jeep and covered her body with it. Still, she was shivering. Akbar had a surge of passion and desire within him but was afraid to touch her body. He really longed to hug her and spend the night on the bed of dried leaves under the tree, but did not have the courage, for a sexual assault on her. He pulled out the shawl from her buttocks and covered her tightly and then his hands deliberately pressed her breast. He became insane with a burning sex desire and leered at her, with lustful and fiery eyes. But, in the darkness she did not see his livid face. He earnestly yearned, that she would respond favourably, for a wild and animal like union of two bodies, but nothing happened. She sat motionless in the darkness, with both eyes closed. Akbar stood looking at her with surging passions, for some time and then went to his driver seat and settled down there, in anger and despair. Time ticked away and the howling and trumpeting, slowly faded away. They heard the sweet music of a lark from a nearby tree heralding the arrival of dawn.

They did not sleep that night even though Jahanara was sitting with eyes closed. At the crack of dawn, they got down from the jeep and went in search of a house to get an axe. Akbar cut some branches of the tree and made way for the jeep to pass through and escaped from the trap. Jahanara thanked God, for saving her life, from wild animals. She thanked Akbar Khan, for his devotion to duty and loyalty, in the face of crisis and also for protecting her from the dangers of forest.

` Akbar, where did that elephant go? I thought it may come and attack us any time.' Jahanara said when the jeep was running at high speed.

`Madam, a herd of elephant will never attack human beings. They will keep on walking, eating and destroying crops and plants on its trail. They will cover 30 to 40 KMs daily. A tusker roaming freely in the forest is very dangerous but, tiger, bison and bear are equally dangerous, as tuskers. We are really lucky to escape from wild animals. Hereafter, we should avoid visiting Hassan estate in the evening and don't linger there upto midnight.' Akbar said.

`OK, Akbar, night journey is to be avoided in future.'

The maids looked at them with suspicion when they arrived in the morning. They sniggered at them when they came to the kitchen, with fatigue on their faces, due to lack of sleep.

`Thatha, we went to Mysore to see my bapa who is not well' Jahanara said.

`Your bapa had called here, during night and wanted to speak to you.' Beevi said with a sneer on her face.

`We were there at that time and his memory is not correct.' Jahanara gave an evading reply and went out with a smile.

A new field officer named Mohsin took charge, in the Spices board and he paid a visit to Jahanara's house. He was her classmate, in High School. He made a suggestion to Jahanara, for starting cardamom cultivation, in their estate. For this purpose, he offered to sanction a huge long term loan of 20 lakhs, with 20% subsidy. There was about 10 acres of marshy field in her estate. He informed her, that the unused fallow land can be transformed, into arable land and cardamom can be cultivated. It would fetch a good profit, annually.

Jahanara agreed for the proposal and applied for the loan. She promptly set out to work on the project. The shrubs, weeds and reeds in the area were completely cleared and the marshy area was filled with sand and then levelled. There was a hillock in the estate and the same was razed for this purpose. Shade trees were planted first in the developed areas. The land was watered and then cardamom seedlings were planted. Sprinklers were erected for the purpose of irrigation. The cardamom plants grew up rapidly, with the special type of manure and pesticides prescribed by the Spices board. An oven for drying cardamom was also constructed, as per the specifications of the field officer.

Jahanara became very close with Mohsin and he began to visit her frequently. He used to visit the cardamom field, along with Jahanara and spend hours among the growing plants. Mohsin taught her how to care the plants and pluck the seeds. He told her that vipers will be seen under the plants and the workers should be made aware of the dangers. If pesticide reaches the foot of the plants, the menace of snakes can be checked to certain extent. Cardamom plants began to flourish, but it took about one year for the first bloom to appear. Tiny buds appeared at the bottom of the plants in hundreds and after pollination small pods appeared. It was an enchanting sight. There will be a special aroma in cardamom fields and this will attract snakes.

On a visit to the cardamom field, Mohsin advised her to plant grampoo (clove) and nutmeg in fallow lands and pepper creepers on the existing shade trees. But, Jahanara did not show any interest in such crops except pepper. She decided to plant pepper plants at the foot of shade trees. Pepper creepers will climb on the shade trees and without much efforts a good profit can be made. But, other crops like grampoo, nutmeg etc will take time to blossom. Another crop is vanilla, but we cannot ensure a steady income from this crop. During conversation, Mohsin casually made enquiries about her personal life.

`Jahanara, I didn't ask you anything about your husband. Where is he now? Where are your children?'

`Mohsin, I expected this question from you. My husband is in jail now. We had a quarrel and he in a fit of anger slapped triple talaq on me and stabbed me in my stomach. It is with the grace of Allah, I escaped from death. The court found him guilty and sentenced him for 5 years. He is now in Parappana Agrahara jail. I've two daughters and they are studying for medicine at Bangalore.' Jahanara said in a sad tone.

`Has he got another wife?' Mohsin asked.

`Yes, there is a lady at Kotagiri. I don't know much about her. My brothers said that she was a distant relative of Tipu Sultan. '

`Is it so; Tipu's relatives are in Calcutta. The relatives of last Mughal emperor Bahadur Shah were also dumped in Calcutta, by the British. They are living like ordinary people doing menial jobs.'

`The emperors and kings have done so much atrocities and their progenies are suffering for their heinous deeds.'

`It is true. The power and pelf are short lived. Some people enjoyed their lives to the maximum and the retribution fell on the head of the blood relations.'

` Mohsin, you did not tell me anything about your personal life.' Jahanara said.

`I've one son and he is in 7th standard. His mother died some three years ago. She was a teacher in a convent.'

Mohsin's eyes became wet and he concealed his grief with a smile.

Mohsin did not ask further questions. They walked back to the estate bungalow, talking and laughing, unmindful of the surroundings and suddenly Akbar Khan happened to see them. Akbar Khan was returning after a trip to his house and he abruptly stopped the jeep. When he saw Mohsin walking with Jahanara in a jovial mood, his face darkened and talked to Mohsin in an insulting way.

`This man is coming here frequently. What is the business with him?'

Mohsin did not like his body language and talk of Akbar Khan.

`Akbar, you are the driver and don't interfere in my job. I'll come here according to my whims and fancies. It is none of your business.' Mohsin retorted.

`It is I who brought you hear .Now you are trying to lure and trap my madam.'

`What trapping. I'll do my services to my client as long as she does not object.'

Jahanara's face became livid with anger, on hearing the talk of Akbar Khan.

`Akbar stop it. Who are you to question him? He is my classmate and close to my family.'

`If you are close with him, marry him.'

It was a bolt from the blue. Mohsin left the place immediately in anger and indignation. Jahanara was very much upset in the impertinent and arrogant remark of Akbar Khan.

On another occasion, the coffee trader Mustapha came to meet Jahanara. Akbar Khan was standing outside, in the porch.

`Where is madam?' Mustapha asked.

`If you have any need tell me. She is busy and no need of meeting her.' Akbar interrupted.

`I came to see madam and not you. Who are you to question me? Call madam now itself.

`She is not here. Vacate the place without barking'. Akbar shouted.

Mustapha became angry in his remark and shouted back.

`You are only a dog, here. Barking is your job. If you play with me, you will know who I'm.' Mustapha retorted.

Hearing the commotion, Jahanara came out.

`Madam, this rascal is threatening me. I want 5 tons of coffee immediately. Can you give it?'

`Of course. There is plenty of coffee in godown. You can come and take it '.

`OK, madam, thank you very much. You have to take action against this rascal. He is misbehaving to the customers. What is his motive? He is trying to blackmail you and trying to tarnish your image. Don't keep him here, any longer' Mustapha said in excited tone.

`All people say you are a womanizer and rogue. I'll not allow you to do business with my madam.' Akbar said.

`Madam has offered to give me one truck load and you are nobody to stop it. I'll come with a truck and if you dare stop it, do it.' Mustapha left with a warning to Akbar.

Within an hour, Mustapha came with a lorry and labourers and loaded coffee, paid the approximate cost and left.' Akbar was not found anywhere, there.

`Mustapha, sorry for the impertinence. If he continues like this, I'll have to replace him with somebody else.' Jahanara apologised.

`OK, madam, thank you for your magnanimity.' Mustapha thanked her and left with the load.

One day, the planter's association secretary Jalappa and two others came to enroll Jahanara in Lions club, but she declined politely. When they left, Akbar Khan came to her and said. ` Madam, do you know this Jalappa? He is a dreaded criminal and don't trust him. He is running an Engineering College at Bangalore. There was a case regarding indiscipline of a student and the student was brutally murdered by some of his goons. The police arrested the goons and he was spared. Don't mingle with such people.'

`How do you know these details? He came here to enroll me in Lions club, but I declined.'

`Don't take membership in such associations. Their work is conducting eye camps and arranging liquor parties in the night.' Akbar said with disdain.

`Let them conduct anything. Why do you worry about it?' Jaharana said.

`What they do is un-Islamic and still many Muslims have taken membership in that club. There are plenty of Kodavas in that club because they like drinking and dancing. We are not like that'.

`They are doing a lot of charitable works. You don't know anything about it'.

`Rafeeque sir was a member and has spent many nights in liquor parties.'

`Akbar don't worry about it. There are many clubs and associations here. Why do you investigate unnecessary things?' Jahanara raised her voice.

`You are a Muslim lady and it is not correct to associate with such organizations. Muslim ladies should use burqa with hijab, but you are walking like a Hindu lady in sari or churidar, without even a headscarf. This is un-Islamic and haram. Even liquor is haram for Muslims and Rafeeque sir was very fond of hot drinks. '

`OK, is there anything else to advise me?'

Jahanara became fed up with Akbar Khan and she called him to her side and advised.

`Akbar, you are living as a member of this house. Why do you behave as an insane person?

Many people are coming here to see me and you are trying to insult them. If you repeat this I'll be constrained to send you home. This is only a warning. Try to improve yourself and behave properly.'

`If you dismiss me, I'll spoil your life I know all your secrets.'

`Are you threatening me? What'll you do if I dismiss you?' Jahanara asked.

`I'll tell the whole world that you are a whore and harlot' Akbar said in highly excited tone.

`Then, you go and broadcast that I'm a bad woman. You have no place here. You get out'. Jahanara shouted at him.

Akbar looked terrified. He lingered there for some time and left with downcast eyes.

Jahanara was in great mental agony for few days. She thought that he would come back, but that did not happen. After one week, she dialled Mustapha and wanted the service of a driver. Next day, a middle aged man named Sebastian reported for duty as driver. After two weeks, Akbar Khan appeared from somewhere and he spoke to Sebastian in a taunting way.

`I 'm the driver; who are you to do my duty.'

Sebastian was embarrassed and he called madam.

Jahanara appeared and shouted at Akbar Khan.

`Your services have been terminated. You have no business here. Get out of my house'

Akbar Khan, went inside and spoke to the maids in the kitchen ` Thatha, this lady is a slut and whore. She has slept with many people. Now, she has many new friends from Kodavas and Muslims. For speaking this truth, she has dismissed me. She'll ruin herself. She has many paramours like Mohsin, Mustapha, and Jalappa etc. etc. I was dismissed since I spoke the truth. She will get the deserving punishment from Allah, without much delay. Really she should be killed by stoning, for adultery.' Akbar shouted.

Jahanara and Sebastian heard everything patiently and did not reply.

Akbar left the house after ten minutes with a warning and curse to Jahanara ` you'll be struck by lightning or bit by viper for dismissing me.'

`OK, if I'm a sinner, let Allah give me the deserving punishment and I'm ready to accept it. '

Jahanara was very much offended in the remarks of Akbar Khan and she stood like a statue without saying anything further. Akbar went back silently. Sebastian was really startled and disturbed in the behaviour of Akbar Khan.

`Sebastian, he has been tormenting me for quite a long time. I suffered silently and finally I was compelled to remove him from service. I hope you'll be obedient. Don't make any problems like him. He is the son of my bapa's friend, but his behaviour is very bad.'

`OK madam, I won't create any problem.' Sebastian said.

`Where is your house?'

`I belong to Mananthavady, Kerala, near the house of Mustapha sir.'

`If you have any problem, please tell me. I've helped Akbar, financially on many occasions and still he is ungrateful. It is I who met the whole expenditure of his elder sister's marriage. I was planning to conduct the marriage of the younger sister also. But, by that time he became my enemy. Sebastian, I hope and pray that you'll be more responsible.'

`OK madam, I'll do my level best to help you.'

`OK, thank you.' Then, Jahanara wiped her tears with the shawl and went inside.

@@@@@@@

8. The tragic death of Akbar Khan.

Two weeks have passed after the dismissal of Akbar Khan. New driver, Sebastian was very punctual in his duties. He will remain in the estate till night, did all kinds of works and reduced the workload of Jahanara. He was staying in a lodge, near the town and Jahanara arranged an accommodation for him, in the vacant quarter of Chandrappa, supervisor, who retired, recently. One day, Sebastian saw Akbar Khan coming through the road, towards the estate with a plastic cover in his hand. Sebastian was going to the Hassan estate, with some bags of manure and packets of pesticides. After returning from Hassan, he told this matter to madam, but she did not take it seriously.

Next day, the workers found the body of Akbar Khan, hanging from the branch of a tree, inside the estate. The sight was horrible. His eyes were open and slightly projected outside. The mouth was open and the tongue fully protruded outside .This was first located by some ladies, who were adding manure to the ginger. One of them ran to the bungalow and informed Jahanara. She was terrified and immediately dialled her brothers. Within one hour, Jaleel and Nazar reached there and consoled Jahanara.They found out the phone number of Akbar Khan's house and informed them about the tragic incident. Then, they informed the local police station. Within half an hour the police party arrived on the spot. A large crowd had gathered in the road and estate compound.

The dead body was examined by police, lowered it after cutting the noose and inquest was conducted. After that, it was covered in a mat and sent for postmortem. They spoke with the eyewitnesses and other people collected over there .After that, the Inspector and party came to meet Jahanara. She was grief-stricken, after hearing the news. When the police party came to the house, Jahanara came out to talk to them. They asked a lot of questions, regarding Akbar Khan. Jaleel and Nazar gave them all necessary information, regarding name, age, address, phone number details of family members, total service in the estate, reason for dismissal etc.

`Why did you dismiss him?' Inspector questioned Jahanara.

`He was like a family member and was very helpful and co-operative. Recently we observed a change in his behaviour. He began to insult our guests and other people who came to the house. We hoped that he'll improve after some time. But, he became arrogant and spoke very rudely and disrespectfully. I warned him several times. But, he did not improve and hence his services were terminated and another driver appointed.'

`What is the reason for his change?'

`I don't know '.

`People say that you had an affair with him. Is it true?'

`No, it is not true. Due to jealousy, people will say cooked up stories. There is no truth in it.'

`Have you got any suicide note?'

`He didn't come here after the new driver joined duty.'

`Is it a suicide or murder?'

`Why should we murder him? I think it is suicide and not murder.'

Then, they called witnesses and took their statements. Also, the maids and the new driver were also questioned and their statements recorded. When they were about to go, Jaleel gave a cover and they accepted it.

At this time, the brother- in-law of Akbar Khan came to the house with one of his friends. He was in a gloomy state and stood outside. Then, Nazar approached him and invited him inside.

`The body has been sent to the hospital for postmortem. The police formalities have been completed just now and they returned to the station.'

`I'm Siddique, brother-in-law of Akbar. I'm coming from Bangalore. They are very much upset and worried.' Siddique said.

`We will accompany the body to Gundlupet. You better go and make arrangements there for funeral ceremony. Inform all relatives to reach there by 4 pm.' Jaleel said.

Siddique and friend left the house after half an hour.

After postmortem, the body was transported to his house at Gundlupet by Jaleel and Nazar. Jaleel explained everything to his relatives gathered there and arranged the burial and follow up rituals. The parents and sisters of Akbar Khan were grief - stricken and still they did not ask any embarrassing questions. While returning home, Jaleel gave a cover containing five thousand rupees to his father and he accepted it without any objection.

Jahanara was laid up for one week, with grief and tension. She felt a kind of guilty conscience and she believed that she was responsible for his suicide. She wanted to visit the house of Akbar and console his parents, in their irreparable loss. But, her maids and brothers advised her not to go there. They feared insulting or humiliating remarks from them. She asked Jaleel to go there again and do all possible help to that family.

After one month, Jaleel went to the police station and met the Inspector and other policemen at the station and made enquiries about the case of Akbar Khan.

`The postmortem report is problem free. No injury, bruises or wounds have been detected on the body. The viscera report also is harmless. No traces of poison, drug or medicine have been found out.' The policeman who had prepared the mahazar told him.

` What is your assessment of the case?' Jaleel asked.

`Enquiry is still going on .We are yet to arrive at a final decision whether to treat it as a suicide or not. One thing is sure, that there is no evidence to treat it as murder. If no other evidence is obtained, we can close the case as suicide.'

`OK sir, thank you for the information?'

`There is nothing to worry. If the case is closed as suicide, we will let you know.' The policeman informed him

`Thank you sir'.

Jaleel returned to Jahanara's house and informed her about the present status of the case. When they were talking a procession came to the house and they stopped at the gate and started shouting slogans.

`Inquilab Zindabad. Inquilab Zindabad. Arrest Jahanara Beevi for the brutal murder of Akbar Khan. Akbar Khan Zindabad.Akbar Khan Zindabad. Give a compensation of 10 lakhs to the family of Akbar Khan, Jahanara Beevi Murdabad. Arrest all the culprits involved in this case. Arrest all the criminals who helped Jahanara. Arrest all the goons of Jahanara Beevi. Inquilab Zindabad. Jahanara Murdabad.'

Jaleel went to the gate and observed. About 30 people had assembled over there and they were shouting slogans. They did not carry any flags of political parties. All of them sat down and their leader began to address them.

`Dear friends, Akbar Khan was a poor driver. He has been serving in this house, for over 5 Years. He was part and parcel of this house. He has two sisters and old parents to look after. As you are aware, Rafeeque sir was more humane and loving. The present owner Madam Jahanara has been tormenting him for more than one year. She is a lusty, amorous witch. She is also very cruel and inhuman. She is a woman of loose virtue. She wanted sex every day. Since he was not willing for that, he was threatened, intimidated, dismissed and finally murdered with her goons. .The police was bribed by her and they are going to close the case as suicide. It cannot be permitted. We want a fresh enquiry and probe by CID or CBI. The guilty should not go scotch free. She should be arrested and sent to jail. We've prepared a lengthy memorandum to our respected CM, Home

Minister, and DGP. We'll never allow her to escape. She should be given exemplary punishment. She should be sent to gallows.'

When his speech came to an end, the slogan shouting started again for about 30 minutes.

Then, the leader came to the house, to meet Jahanara.

`Madam, I'm a local leader. We've formed a Joint Action Council, to find out the real culprits in the brutal murder of our comrade Akbar Khan. We've prepared a lengthy memorandum to our CM, HM and DGP. Shall I read it out to you?. We won't allow the police to close the case as suicide. It is really a murder planned and executed by you, by your goons in the estate. We've got clear evidence of the conspiracy behind that and full details of the culprits.'

`OK, what is your name?' Jahanara asked.

`I'm Raja Gowda and I belong to the ruling party. I'm also running an NGO for the emancipation of the poor, downtrodden, under -privileged, sidelined, oppressed and suppressed people.' Gowda said.

`OK, good thing; why did you come to meet me?' Jahanara asked.

`Madam, shall I read out the memorandum or if you want I shall give a copy of the same to you. ' Gowda asked.

`No, thanks. Joint action council is comprised of which parties?'

` It is comprised of ruling party and opposition.'

`OK, it is a good thing. What shall I do for you?' Jahanara asked.

`Madam, we are prepared to settle the issue amicably, if you give us Rupees 20 lakhs. Out of this, we will give some amount as compensation to the house of the deceased.'

`You can't blackmail me. I won't give a single rupee. If I'm guilty, send me to gallows. Get out '.

`If you don't agree, you will have to pay heavy price. You will be in jail for the rest of your life'.

`You are a cheat and criminal. You are trying to make money, by blackmail and treachery. Don't stand here, you   clear out, I say. You can't blackmail me. You are trying to get defame me, by false allegations. Get out of my house'? Jahanara roared.

He was terrified, walked out of the house and slowly moved to the gate. Within 5 minutes, the meeting was dispersed.

After one week, an Innova car came to the house and some colourfully dressed people got down with movie cameras, still cameras, camera stands, mikes etc.

On hearing doorbell, Jahanara came out.

`Madam, we are from local and national channels.' One of them said.

`We are going to give a feature about you in our channels.' Another person said.

`What feature?'

`You've become famous with one murder. We want to interview you and take some photos in still and movie cameras. Hope you've no objection.'

`I've objection. I don't want unnecessary fame and publicity. All of you please get out, I say.' Jahanara shouted.

`Madam, it is for your good. You can say your version, in the interview.'

`No, I don't want your help. Please clear out, now itself.'

All of them went out of the house, boarded the car and left.

After a few days, a tall and bearded person with a bag came to the house. Jahanara invited him and gave him a seat in the porch.

`Madam, I'm Bellari Sathianathan. I'm a film director. Recently, I read a lot about your driver and his sensational murder. There is a serial in the local channel similar to this story. The wife of a rich man loved the driver and enjoyed life with him for years, secretly. The husband came to know about the infidelity of his wife and decided to kill both of them .Later, he'd a second thought to spare his wife, since he feared that his children would suffer, in the absence of mother. He engaged a professional killer for the job, by paying Rs 20 lakhs. The owner asked the driver to take his friends to the forest, to take some wild photographs and he obeyed. The leader and his gang boarded the car, befriended the driver and went to a lake near the forest. They asked the driver to stop and all of them got out with their cameras .The driver did not have even a tinge of suspicion, about their intention. Within a minute, they pushed the car into the lake. With money and influence, the case was treated as accident and case closed. The wife spoke against her lover and said to the police that he was suffering from epilepsy for a long time and his death is nothing but an accident. I've directed three films and I would like to depict your story also. If you cooperate with me, a beautiful film can be produced about your eventful life. It will definitely run for minimum 100 days. It'll be a big box-office success. A millionaire marries a lovely and angelic widow whose mother's grandmother's grandfather was a Sultan. He, later divorces his real wife by triple talaq and tries to kill her. That faithful and loving lady becomes revengeful. She loves her driver and sleeps with him and thus settle scores with her cruel and unfaithful husband. She, later becomes a Cleopatra and entertains many lovers at a time. This infuriates the first lover and he quarrels with her and deserts her. He tells the world about her sexual encounters and adventures and this leads to his brutal and heinous murder.'

Sathianathan said in brief the story of his next film.

`What shall I do for this?'

`I've some doubts and you have to clear it '

`What is that?' Jahanara asked.

`Have you seen the lady who claimed to be a relative of the sultan?'

`No. '

`Is she beautiful?'

`Get out. You nasty beggar, get out of my house.' She shouted.

Bellary Sathianathan stood up and took to his heels.'

When he went, Jahanara began to sob. She could not control her grief; she went to her room and fell to the bed.

`These wretched people are mocking at me and making my life a hell. I'll never bend my head before these scoundrels. I had done too much for Akbar and he made me a whore. I'm helping all my maids and workers and treat them as equals and they take pleasure in my misfortune and distress. I saw a smirk on the faces of Beevi and Fatima' she said to herself.

A yellow newspaper of Mysore, had printed and published fantastic and sensational stories about Jahanara and her lover Akbar Khan. The story depicted Jahanara as an ambitious lady of insatiable sex desire and she used her driver Akbar Khan for this purpose, for over one year. She was also in love with a lot of other high profile people, in the society. When Akbar was found to be a hurdle for her freedom and for keeping her secrets, he was eliminated by her goons in the estate. People began to look at her with fear and disgust.

Jahanara spent two weeks in her room in anger and despair. The maids brought food and other things to her room and she noticed a smirk on their faces, always. She felt dejected and depressed in the behaviour of people who find pleasure in the grief of others. She granted free leave to Sebastian and lay in bed, in rambling thoughts. Despite the misfortune and scandal she was stoical and never repented for anything. Her parents and brothers came to her house and spent there for one week.

`Umma, my time is very bad and hence I'd to suffer a lot of criticism and scandal from the staff and public. But, I'll never stoop before anybody. All are cheats and nobody can be trusted, in this world.' Jahanara complained to her mother in tears.

`You cool down. Nothing has happened to you to moan like a dog. You should be courageous and face the enemies with confidence and determination. Nothing will happen to you.' Mother advised her.

`Umma, I want to do namaz daily. For quite a long time I'd no time and patience for praying to Allah. From today onwards, I'll do namaz, regularly.'

`Only in adversity people will remember Allah. I've brought two namaz dresses. You can take one and wear it and do namaz, now itself. Just now I heard the call from the mosque.'She said.

Jahanara wore the white mantle over her churidar, covered her head with a scarf and sat down to pray with a holy Quran in hand. She first did namaz and then began reading Quran. She felt relief from her tension and worry. She forgot her estate, house, children and everything and spent days in complete penance and prayers. Her parents spent with her one week and returned to their house.

After two weeks, Jahanara rose from the deep chasm of anguish and mental agony and became cheerful and confident, as before. She made a trip to Hassan with driver Sebastian .Nobody looked at her with any kind of prejudice or dislike. She had a call from Mohsin and she spoke to him cheerfully as before. The dark clouds of anxiety and worry have vanished from her life.

@@@@@@@

9. Rafeeque gets his first parole

After one year, Rafeeque applied for parole for one month, on health reasons and the same was granted. He went direct to the Kotagiri estate and settled down in the estate bungalow. He had a shower in cold water and dinner from the Paradise hotel .Night was very chilly and he slept comfortably the whole night under the blanket. Next morning, Saira Bhanu came to meet him and invited him to her house, but he declined. Food was brought from the hotel as the previous day. Saira Bhanu is now financially self-reliant with her income from the job. She expressed her boundless love and gratitude to her mentor and benefactor, Rafeeque Sir.'

`Sir, I'd received a letter from my mother. They came to know about the demise of Freddy only now. There is a teacher in my beti's High School, from Calcutta. Recently, she had paid a visit to her house in Calcutta and also met my brother, who is running a shop, near her house, at Cossipore.

They may come to meet me and my daughter, shortly.'

`It is a good news and I find it difficult to believe. When will they come? Rafeeque asked.

`Date not decided yet.'

`I'll go back to jail after one month. Before that, I've to visit Ajmer Dargah Sharif. I had taken a vow to visit that place, when I heard that Jahanara has survived the attack. I believe in Sufi saints also.'

`Sir, faith in god almighty is always good for peace of mind. I do believe in god, even though I did not practice my religion, after marriage. Freddy was an atheist and communist. He did not believe in God and religion and any other ism other than communism. He is really a great thinker and humanitarian, but he became an addict to liquor.' Saira Bhanu extolled Freddy.

`Was he a member of the communist party?'

`No, he was only a supporter. He was not in the habit of visiting churches or holy places. He gave me full freedom to practice my religion. I continued as Muslim even after marriage, even though I did not practice it. My daughter Jessinda has not been baptised. He said ` let her select any religion she likes, when she becomes grown up'. He was really a revolutionary. He used to say that it was by chance or accident we were born as Hindu, Muslim and Christian etc. We had no choice to select our religion. We must learn to live as human beings first and no need of fighting in the name of religion and faith.' Saira said.

`Will you go to Calcutta to see all of your relatives and friends?'

`I've not decided. After eloping with Freddy, I've not been to Calcutta and seen my Maa and others.'

`What about Freddy's relatives?'

`Nothing is known about them. His brother was a doctor and Freddy was teaching in a private college, there. His father was an officer in the Gun and Shell factory, Cossipore, Calcutta and he belonged to Howrah. His grandfather was an Englishman and after independence, he remained in Calcutta till his death and was buried in a cemetery, there. It is not known whether

Freddie's mother is alive or not. I was studying for II year of LLB, at South Calcutta Law College, when we met each other, in the library, near our house. Even though, he was our neighbour, I was meeting him for the first time. I liked him and loved him at the first sight. This news spread like wildfire and reached the ears of my mother, brothers and relatives. The fanatics raised alarm and took up arms to kill us. They came to our house and threatened me and asked my mother to stop my study. But, threats and intimidations could not prevent us from meeting each other. We took a hard decision to run away from that place to the south. They came behind us and searched the Railway station, bus stand, ferry etc, but failed to locate us. We had anticipated this and hid in a friend's house, for one week and boarded a train to Chennai from Howrah station. Later, we moved to Ooty for security reasons and found out a job for Freddy, in a tea estate at Coonoor. I was in the grip of fear for about one month and did not try for any job. This is my eventful and poignant story. There is scope for a good film'

`A graduate and law student came to work as maid. It is really surprising.' Rafeeque said.

`It is better than begging. It is your timely help that sustained us. I've seen people living as worms in Calcutta city and suburbs. Have you read the famous novel - The city of Joy? ` Lakhs of refugees from Bangladesh flow to Calcutta, every month and live in most filthy and unhygienic conditions, in hovels. The entire Bengalis show sympathy towards them irrespective of religion. Our Jyothi Babu is from East Bengal and he showed great sympathy and love towards these hapless peoples. Many people've told me about their mind wrenching stories. Some people make publicity in their villages that they'll get milk and honey in Calcutta city and they cross over to India, through the porous border. They are caught by BSF and released after removing valuables and money. They travel to Calcutta in penniless conditions and spends days without food and sleep on footpath. In Calcutta, there are many people who give them all kinds of support like food, money, shelter and even forged documents to live in India. Calcutta is really a city of joy and many of these refugees end up in brothels, Sonaganj or some other brothels. Calcutta is suffocating with these refugees, but they won't drive them out'. Saira Bhanu narrated the story of Bangladeshis.

When she went home, Cherian and PRO came for discussion.

`Cherian, how is our overdraft?'

`We have paid back about 10 lakhs. There is nothing to worry. We are getting more work from small holders. Company is running on good profit.'

`How is our workers? Do they raise any new demands?'

`No sir, they are very cooperative in all respects. Our workers are exemplary. Did you hear about the problem of Moopanar estate?'

`No, what is the problem?'

`Moopanar, the managing partner was a dictator and he treated his workers as slaves. A kind of bonded labour existed there. The workers suffered for a long time and then they revolted and the estate was locked out by the management. It ended in permanent closure of the estate. They conducted several litigations, dialogues and discussions to end the labour problem, but in vain. The workers were adamant and they did not mind even the court directives. The management could not open the estate even after the intervention of the state government The RDO came and met the union representatives and assured them that justice will be done. He later sought the help of Labour commissioner to end the labour dispute. Labour commissioner tried his level best, for an amicable solution, but failed due to the noncooperation of workers. The tea plants have become shrubs and trees, due to non-plucking and pruning of tea leaves. The factory remained closed, for a long time without maintenance, and the machinery has rusted fully. The workers are in hunger and famine. Some workers have found temporary jobs, in other plantations. Some workers are cutting the shade trees, one by one and carrying them to the market and selling them as firewood for livelihood.' PRO narrated the story in detail.

`By the by, Cherian I 'm going on a pilgrimage to Ajmer Dargah, tomorrow. I'll catch a flight from Coimbatore to New Delhi and from there to Jaipur. From Jaipur, I'll go by bus or cab. I'll stay there for a couple of days and return. Please arrange a vehicle and driver to take me at 6 am, tomorrow to Coimbatore Airport.

`OK sir, we'll arrange it.' Cherian promised.

 After half an hour, they wound up the discussion and parted.

Rafeeque started the journey at 6 am and reached Jaipur by 2 pm. After lunch, boarded a bus and reached Ajmer by evening. He took a room in a luxury hotel in the city, had a bath, dinner and went to sleep. Next day, at 8.30 am, he reached the Dargah. Outside and inside of the Dargah was filled with crowd of pilgrims belonging to various communities. Rafeeque thought Hindu ladies outnumbered all others. In the compound, he saw a familiar face and it was his friend Devaiah.

`Sir, it is a surprise and I never expected you here. It is my luck or good fortune that I could meet you here. Are you alone?' Rafeeque enquired.

`Yes, I 'm alone. For the last two months, I was on pilgrimage. Even gods have deserted me '

Devaiah was in grief and despair.

` Sir, when did you come here?'

`I'm here for the last one week. I've not decided what to do next or where to go'. He said in a voice choked with emotion, grief and disappointment.

`Sir, what is the problem to be so desperate and unhappy.' Rafeeque enquired.

`Rafeeque, I'll come to your hotel today and I've to tell you a lot of things.'

`OK, I'll go inside now, complete the prayers and come back'

`OK, complete the rituals and come back. I'll wait for you here.'

 It took more than one hour to complete the prayers and rituals. Rafeeque closed his eyes and sat silent on the floor covering his head with a scarf, for about half an hour and then went and received the blessings and prasad. When he came out of the shrine, Devaiah was standing near the exit.

`Today, there are more pilgrims than yesterday. I'm staying here for the last two days. My mind is still like a boiling kettle. I tried to cool it by fanning and pouring cold water over it, but in vain' Devaiah told Rafeeque when he was walking along with him to the hotel.

`Sir, where is your hotel?' Rafeeque enquired.

`Rafeeque, I'm staying in an ordinary hotel. It is on the parallel road.

Rafeeque and Devaiah sat in the foyer of the hotel and started talking.

`Rafeeque, have you patience and presence of mind to hear what I say?' Devaiah said.

`Yes, of course. I 'm very much worried and perturbed about you. Tell me your problems without any hesitation.'

`My wife passed away, some three months back. Before dying, I arranged the marriage of my sons, as requested by her. Both the daughter- in- laws are from average families. They are fair and lovely. It was their choice and I didn't object. My sons have to look after their families also.

Before dying, she called me by her side and said in feeble voice. 'If I die, there'll be nobody to look after you. So, please promise that you will marry my cousin Maya. Don't wait for the permission of my sons. They are selfish and will never be on good terms with you. She asked me to call Maya and when she came, she took her hand and gave it to me and said 'This is your companion in my absence. Look after her and her son. Let god be with you.' She said in tears.

She died peacefully, the following day. It was a bolt from the blue and I found it difficult to control my grief and anguish.I wept like a woman, in the loss of my beloved wife. She was with me in thick and thin and never blamed me in anything. I've not cheated her even in thought and not scolded or admonished her. She was so dear and near to me. During the war, it was her words that gave me courage and encouragement. She'll write letters daily to console me-'I'm praying for you and nothing will happen to you. If gods could not protect you and you got killed, I'll consider it a boon or blessing. It is a great thing to die for our motherland. It is a blessing for the family and we'll take pride in your martyrdom.'

There was no problem in the house till the completion of the final ceremony. Maya was everywhere and she did everything in the place of a mother. But, when the rites and rituals came to an end , she became superfluous and unwanted, to my sons and daughter- in -laws. They planned and conspired to get rid of her and it was executed in my absence. They spread a rumour that some money kept in the shelf was found missing and tried to put the blame on her. She was an innocent type and did not respond. They did not relish her attitude and behaviour towards me. Every morning she'll come to my room and wake me up and bring morning coffee to my bed. She'll prepare hot water for my bath and wash my clothes herself etc.

That day, I'd gone to Mysore to meet a friend. They took her and her son in our car and dropped them in her house and returned home. When I returned from Mysore, she and her son were found missing and on enquiry my daughter- in- laws told me that she was dropped at her house at Mysore, since no maid was required in this house, after Amma's demise.

Immediately, I went to her house and met her. She was in tears, for the harassment meted out to her, by his sons and daughter-in- laws. I could not control myself and I took her and her brother to the sub registry office and registered our marriage, then and there. After that, I took her back to my home. My sons did not permit her to enter the house. Hence, she waited outside the gate and I went inside, took my belongings and original copy of the land documents and returned to her house, in a shattered state of mind.

`You could have married her on the day of Amma's funeral. Why did you wait for completion of the rites and rituals, to make her your own? This is sacrilege and Amma's soul'll never pardon you. We don't want such a father bereft of any love towards our Maa and us.'

Both of my sons said in unison in the presence of their wives.

`On hearing such taunting and accusing words, my mind became numb and wounded and we ran away from the place, in indignation and disgust. I'd some savings in two banks and I transferred five lakhs to her name, immediately, to make her life secure and happy. I personally went to Virajpet again and collected the TC of her son and admitted him in the English medium school, at Mysore. My sons are in a revengeful mood and have filed a case in the civil court, for partition of ancestral properties. The case is going on and may take years or decades for final judgment. Presently, I 'm living in her house and we have a plan to buy a plot of land in the village and construct a small house. After the demise of my wife, I became an unwanted stuff for my children. I'm a soldier and still I've no place to live in and no peace of mind. When I was in service, I'd visited many holy places in North India. I'd visited Ajmer Dargah once, along with a friend. In North India, Ajmer is a very important tourist cum pilgrim center .Even Hindus and Sikhs believe in Sufi saints and visit this shrine in large numbers. One day, I saw this shrine in dream and decided to spend one week there and pray for peace of mind.' Devaiah narrated the story.

Devaiah was found in a highly depressed and worried state of mind.

`Sir, even though I 'm in jail, I keep my composure. You are a war veteran and still you are broken and shattered like a wooden plank. Be courageous and face the world with grit and determination. How long they will fight against their own father who begetted them? It is nothing but foolishness. Every day, I remember my parents for bringing me up to this stage and making me rich.'

`My sons are selfish in many respects and now they hate their father. If I had not married that lady, my condition would have been very pitiable.'

`Sir, where is your daughter? Does she show any love and sympathy towards her father?' Rafeeque put a question.

`Rafeeque, she is also after ancestral property and has not visited me after the estrangement with her brothers.' Devaiah said.

`How is your son- in- law? His mother is my classmate.'

`He is a nice boy; but financially not up to the mark. He is only a junior advocate and the income from the profession is not much. I advised him to stop practice and write for bank tests. His brothers are well off and they have no connection with his mother, now. She is their step mother.' Devaiah spoke the truth.

`How is your wife? Is she prepared to move to Ooty?' Rafeeque said.

`Have you any plan in my case?'

`Sir, our factory manager is about to retire. I'm in search of an able man for that post.'

`Rafeeque, I'm willing to take up any job. Please consider my case and I'll be grateful to you forever. I'm very much frustrated and had applied for the security officer job in a firm at Mysore.'

`Don't go for such jobs; you are a retired army officer.'

I've been sitting idle for quite a long time and I'm really fed up of life and yearn for a job.' Devaiah entreated.

`OK Sir, I'll consider your case and let you know about it shortly.' Rafeeque promised.

`Thank you, Rafeeque. I'll return, home after visiting Pushkar also.'

`Where is it? I've not heard about such a place.'

`It is a very important pilgrim center and lakhs of people will flock together, at this shrine on some important festivals, like

Karthika, Deepavali, Durga-puja etc. It is on the other side of the hill, towards Jaipur side. It is a wonderful place, with many temples at the top of small hills. There is a temple dedicated to Brahma also, there. There is a big tank and bathing ghats and chambers for pilgrims to rest. I've gone there once, on the eve of Karthika and the whole place was illuminated with tiny oil lamps. After the festival is over, this place will have a deserted look with no pilgrims and shopwallahs.'

`Sir, I'll return tomorrow evening. I'll make another visit to this shrine, tomorrow and then start the return journey.' Rafeeque said.

`OK, Rafeeque, I'll wait for your intimation. Don't forget '.

`Never, I 'm sympathetic towards you and I'll call you, shortly '.

`Thank you Rafeeque.' He stood up and embraced Rafeeque and left to his hotel.

When, Rafeeque returned to Kotagiri, Manager Cherian came to his bungalow.

`Rafeeque sir, Saira Bhanu madam has left the station after submitting her resignation letter. The key of her house also has been handed over to me.'   Cherian said placing the key before him

`She'd told me that her mother and brother will come from Calcutta. I never thought that she'll go with them.'

`Mother did not come. Her brother and wife came and took them back.'

`She was an extraordinary lady. I've not seen such a bold and sincere lady, in my entire life. After break up with my family, I offered to marry her, but she declined. She has told me, her thrilling story of how she and her husband escaped, from the religious fanatics, when she eloped with Freddy. By the by, Cherian, the factory manager Ganapathi will retire this month and I'm planning to take a retired army officer to that post. He is my friend and his name is Maj. Devaiah.'

`OK Sir, I'll do the needful. Please give me his details.'

`If Saira does not come back, we can allot that house to him; since he'll come with family and son needs admission in school. That house is very near to the school and it will be ideal and convenient to them. I may go back by that time and you may take care of that. Keep this key with you and hand over the house to him. Please arrange to clean up the house, with somebody before he arrives.' Rafeeque instructed Cherian.

In the meanwhile, Rafeeque sent a communication to Devaiah and directed him to meet estate manager Cherian, on the last day of that month, so that he can join duty on the 1st of the following month. He had also mentioned that, he was free to bring his family with him, since accommodation has been arranged, near the school. He was also requested to bring TC of the boy with him.

On the last day of the parole, Rafeeque was coming to Kotagiri from Ooty at night; he saw a flash of his old friend, Pramila Devi. She was driving a car, at a moderate speed, in the opposite direction. Immediately, Rafeeque slowed down his car, took reverse and tried to chase the car. But, he could not locate the car. He thought that the car would have turned to an alley. He verified two alleys, but in vain.

In the second alley, he stopped the car and made enquiries with a number of residents.

`Where is the house of Excise Commissioner?'

`What is his name?'

`I don't know his name. He is a rich and influential man .His wife's name is Pramila Devi.'

`There is no such commissioner here. This road leads to a colony of criminals and mafias. If you don't know his name, don't roam here, unnecessarily. Just now a stab case occurred here and the police are searching for the accused.' One of the locals warned him. Rafeeque was terrified and he reversed the vehicle and went to his estate, immediately.

Rafeeque returned to the jail after completion of parole period. When he reached the jail, one letter was found in the letter box and he opened it with anxiety.

Dear Rafeeque sir,

My brother and family had come to Kotagiri, when you were away to Ajmer and on their compulsion, I have resigned my job and taken TC of my daughter. My daughter has been admitted to an English medium school, near our house. Also I am happy to inform you that, I have rejoined my old Law College, for completion of the LLB course. The principal objected that it can't be permitted after such a long break and I had to obtain special sanction from the university. Then, how are you? How was your journey to Ajmer? I hope and pray for your happiness and wellbeing. You have been very kind and considerate towards me and my daughter, when we were in distress. I regret deeply that you are suffering a jail term, because of me. I hope, Allah who is omnipotent, omnipresent and almighty, knows your innocence and will show you, the right path in life. I again pray to the almighty, to help you, for early release from jail. Hope your life in the jail is happy and without problems. I hope and pray that you would have reunited with your family ,by this time. With love and regards, Saira Bhanu. Rafeeque read the letter many times and put it below his pillow.

@@@@@@@

10. Jahanara goes through an ordeal

The family of Akbar Khan remained loyal to Jahanara.They earnestly believed that Akbar's death was only suicide. Hence, they neither blamed nor indulged in creating problems for Jahanara. Hence, Jahanara was sympathetic towards that family and paid a handsome amount as compensation, through her brother Jaleel. But, the joint action council decided to proceed with the case and submitted a memorandum to the Chief Minister, Home Minister and DGP and prayed for reinvestigation of the case. Raja Gowda visited the parents of Akbar, but they did not fall in his trap. After six months, the government decided to get it investigated again and issued necessary orders in this regard and handed over the case to CID of police. One day, a policeman from the local police station came to the estate and told Jahanara ` Madam, the government has appointed one DySP Suleiman for reinvestigation of the case and they will start the work, without delay. He has asked me to request you to allot the outhouse, for this purpose'.

`I can't say anything in this regard. I've to contact my brothers' Jahanara said.

`He is coming from Bangalore and it is rather difficult to get an accommodation, in this area .Please obtain permission from your brothers before he arrives.'

`OK, let me try. '

The following day, coffee trader Mustapha came to give the balance amount of the coffee purchased and then Jahanara mentioned this case to him.

`Mustapha, a DySP is coming to reinvestigate the Akbar's case. Have you got anybody in police department to get an idea about this police officer? They have demanded the outhouse also for their stay.'

`If they've made a request, it is better to give it. Otherwise, they'll do more harm to us. I'll collect full details about this man and pass on the information to you shortly.' Mustapha said. He has contact with some politicians of the ruling party and officers in the police department.

After a couple of days, Mustapha informed Jahanara over phone` Madam, this Officer is really a terror and an expert in cracking difficult and intricate cases. He'll not accept any bribe since he is immensely rich. He is very religious and will not drink. His only weakness is girls. He used to say to all his clients about the 3 Ws viz. Wine, women and wealth. He is the son of former Excise

Commissioner and is not in need of money. He'll not take liquor since he is Muslim and for settling matters with the relatives of accused persons, he may demand girls. He'll make loopholes in the charge sheets for easy acquittal of the cases. '

`OK, let him prove the case. We've not done any wrong and we don't require his help. If his intention is to convert the suicide into murder, we will have to question the same in the court. Let us see what is going to happen' Jahanara said.

After two days, a police jeep came to the house and three people came out and met Jahanara.

`I 'm Sulaiman, DySP, CID and others my assistants. Madam, where is the outhouse? I'll be staying here, and others are locals and will go to their houses, in the evening.'

`Be seated, I'll bring tea.'

Jahanara went inside and came with a tray containing four cups of tea and served to them.

`Since there are no hotels in the vicinity, food also may be given to us.'

`OK, I'll arrange it.'

`By the by, we require a list of your workers in the estate 'DySP said.

`OK, I'll collect the details from the supervisors and that also will be given.' Jahanara promised.

`If there are any criminals among them, you've to give the details whether they have been convicted earlier and for what offence etc.'

`No such people here; all are good samaritans'

After tea, they moved to the outhouse.

Jahanara instructed Sultan to take lunch to the policemen at 1 pm.

She prepared a list of the workers and that was given to the DySP. After lunch, all of them went to the estate and verified the tree on which Akbar's body was found hanging and spoke to some of the workers.

Next day, the workers were called to the outhouse and their statements were taken and recorded. All the 26 workers including supervisors were called to the outhouse and questioned. The investigation went on for one month. In the meanwhile, they went to the house of Akbar Khan and took the statements of his parents and sister. The joint action council president Raja Gowda and some other activists were also called to the outhouse and their statements recorded.

Finally, Jahanara was called for questioning. She went to the outhouse along with Beevi. But Jahanara was called inside and Beevi was asked to wait outside.

`It is heard that you are responsible for his murder. Is it true?'

`Why should I kill him? He was my driver for over 5 years. In the recent times, I observed a change in his behaviour towards me and others in the house. On many occasions, he became angry with me and my maids. Some of our guests were also insulted by him. I gave warning many times and still he did not improve and hence he was removed from service and another driver appointed. Akbar tried to quarrel with the new driver also. One day, his body was found hanging in the estate. That day, my new driver had seen him passing through the road with a plastic cover. We have not done anything to provoke him for suicide,' Jahanara explained.

`There is a talk that you'd an affair with him. Is it true?'

`No, it is not true. Some people are jealous and speak ill of us and their words can't be believed.'

`Where is your husband?'

`He is in Parappana Agrahara jail'.

` Is he a convict? What was his crime?'

`He stabbed me with a knife in a fit of anger. He is undergoing imprisonment for 5 years'

`Madam, what is this? You are very wealthy but no peace in your life.'

`It is my fate. I'm helpless.'

`Do you have children and where are they.'

`I've two daughters and they are medical students.'

`My daughter also is studying for medicine.'

`Let me ask you one thing. I feel that he was eliminated by you. He was a nuisance to you and you engaged some goons to strangle him to death and the body was hung from the tree.'

`No sir, it is suicide and not murder.'

`Tell me the truth, who killed him? How much you paid for the goon?'

Jahanara kept mum.

`Who killed him? Tell me the truth or you will be made the first accused. You will have to languish in jail for the rest of your life.'

`I've no hand in his suicide. His dismissal may be the reason for his suicide.'

`I say, it is a murder. He was strangled to death and the body was hung from the tree.'

`I've nothing to say about this.'

 After Jahanara, her maids also were questioned. They affirmed that it was a suicide. Madam has no grudge against him. He lost his job since he was arrogant and started insulting madam and her guests.

`How much did she give you for keeping the secret? You are also a party in the conspiracy. Some people've told me that she was behind the murder. Two workers in the estate are the culprits. They were paid a huge sum by your madam. To keep the secret you were also bribed by her. How much did you get?' He shouted at the top of his voice.

Beevi and Fatimata were frightened by his outbursts and facial expression. But, still they kept on repeating ` it was a suicide and not murder.'

Sulaiman tried his level best to extract the truth from them, but failed.

`I thought you'll cooperate with me, but you are shielding your madam. I'll call you again shortly. If I get credible evidence that it was a murder, you also will become culprits and is likely to get a life term' Sulaiman thundered.

`She is innocent and it is a suicide.' They said in unison.

`You can go now, but I'll call you again.' The DySP reminded him.

Sebastian also was called for questioning the next day.

`What is your name?'

`Where is your house?'

`Mananthavady'

`How did you manage a job here in Kodagu?'

` I was brought here by Mustapha sir, coffee trader.'

`What is the connection with him?'

`He is my friend and neighbour.'

`Do you know this Akbar?'

`I've spoken to him when I came here for the first time.'

`I think you are also involved in the murder."

`No sir, it is only a suicide and murder.'

`How much did you get for saying like this?'

`I'm sure that it is a suicide. That day of his death, I saw him walking through this road with a small cover containing plastic yarn.'

`How did you know that it was plastic yarn?'

` A portion of the plastic yarn was visible outside. He hanged using a plastic yarn.'

`OK, I'll call you again. Now you can go.'

That day Jahanara was completely upset and she remained in her room, with door closed. She spoke to Jaleel and Nazar.

`Jaleel, I'm fed up with his insinuating and insulting questions. What shall I do?'

`Didi, he is trying to demoralise you to extract more information. Anyway, I'm coming and we can discuss the next course of action.'

Jaleel came that evening.

That night, a jeep came to the outhouse and a young girl got down from the jeep and went inside. The jeep went back and the girl remained with the DySP. Jaleel went near the outhouse and observed. He heard giggling of the girl and suppressed talk of the DySP. Beevi went there with dinner and she saw a slim and fair girl sitting in the sofa of the living room.

`I saw a lady with him. I think he is a shameless fellow .He is misusing our outhouse.' Beevi told Jahanara after returning from the outhouse.

`What can we do? He is a police officer. If we did anything to antagonise him, he'll arrest me and put me in jail. The suicide of Akbar will be made murder and that charge will be slapped on my head. They have no such compunction and will do anything with impunity. He can cook up evidence and trap me. Let him do anything he likes and I am not going to complain.' Jahanara babbled.

 At midnight, they heard a sudden scream from the outhouse and after a few minutes, they heard a knock on the door. When the door was opened, they were startled to see a young girl standing at the door crying.

`Who are you, why are you crying?' Jahanara asked.

` I 'm a college student. I came here to request the DySP to save my brother implicated in a murder case.'

`What is your name?' Jahanara asked.

`I 'm Divya from Mysore.'

`What do you want?'

` There is a snake in the house and he was bitten. I ran away from there.'

She was called inside by Jahanara. Jaleel and Sultan went there, with a torch.

The DySP was lying on the floor in a dazed condition; his face had turned bluish. He had a bite on the foot and blood was oozing. They verified the room and found a viper hiding at one corner of the room. Sultan killed it with a stick and the DySP was taken in their car and admitted to the hospital. The snake also was taken to the hospital, in a plastic cover. The doctors examined the snake and administered antivenom injection to the DySP. Jaleel contacted the police station and collected the mobile number of his family and informed his wife about the incident. Next day, his wife and son arrived and Jaleel was relieved of the duty in the hospital and he returned to the house of Jahanara. The condition of DySP continued very serious and in the evening, he was taken to the Bangalore Medical College.

The girl spent that night in Jahanara's house and went home in early morning.

`Divvya, you are lucky and escaped from death, with the grace of God. The snake spared you this time, knowing that you are innocent.'

She embraced Jahanara and sobbed.

`Bahenji, please excuse me for my mistake. I'll never repeat it.'

He remained in the hospital for one week, in critical condition. The venom adversely affected the functioning of both the kidneys and he breathed his last, despite best treatment at the Medical College. Thus, the enquiry was deadlocked for six months. Another DySP from Bangalore under name Ramachandrappa came and restarted the investigation. He took a rented accommodation in the town and completed the probe within one month. The case was treated as suicide and closed. Jahanara heaved a sigh of relief.

Rabia and Zeenath came to Virajpet estate during vacation and spent one month with Jahanara. They insisted their mother to go with them to the jail and meet daddy, but she refused.

`Mama. Please come with us to meet him in the jail .After all, he is our daddy. We want to meet him.'

`Don't you love your mama? If not, go and meet him in jail and don't come to me, thereafter.

I loved him adored him and still he slept with many other ladies. I hate that man and there will be no life with him, till I die.' Jahanara spoke in a highly emotional tone.

`Mama, I can understand your anger and pain. But, he has not done anything wrong to us and he loved us deeply.' Zeenath said.

`Mama, If you don't like it, we'll never compel you for any reconciliation with him.' Rabia whispered.

`If you want to meet him, go and meet him. I'll never raise an objection. 'Jahanara interrupted.

`Mama we can leave that subject. I've to speak to you about an important subject. A Tibetan girl is studying with us in the Medical College. She has invited all of us to her house at Bylakuppe near Kushalnagar. Will you come with us to meet her?' Rabia asked.

`OK, I'll come with you, there. We can plan a trip tomorrow.'

`OK, thank you Mama.'

Jahanara spoke to the driver Sebastian and he agreed for the journey. Next day, they started at 8 in the morning after breakfast and reached there by 9am. On the way, Rabia told Jahanara the painful story of the Tibetan refugees.

`Mama, their country, Tibet was the most peaceful place on the earth. It is called roof of the world and the capital is Lhasa.It was ruled by their Buddha incarnate, Dalai Lama. That place is extremely cold and even trees became stunted. It is said there was no policemen or army in that country because people loved one another and it was a crime free nation. All of a sudden everything turned topsy turvy. They had to flee from that country, leaving everything behind. One day, Chinese army advanced to that country and it was annexed by China.

Dalai Lama and a portion of his followers escaped to India through rocky ravines and meandering gorges in the dead of the night and reached India. They were settled at three or four places in India and one of their settlement is Bylakuppe, in our state. Karnataka government came forward to help them and granted 3000 acres of land for setting up refugee camps .This was later converted into a full-fledged settlement and monastery. The government helped in health care, education and for finding out livelihood.   Now, their population has exceeded one lakh .Each family was provided with land for cultivation.They have done wonders there .This is the second biggest settlement in India. The first place goes to the Dharamtala at Shimla, Himachal Pradesh. For many years they suffered for livelihood and now they are almost settled.

The government of India has not yet granted citizenship to these refugees. In the earlier days they stitched warm clothes and travelled the length and breadth of India for selling them. Now, they are living by means of agriculture and cottage Industries for producing warm clothes. The government has set apart few seats for them in some Engineering and Medical colleges, here.

My friend Sangye is a very intelligent and loving girl and she helps us very much in our studies.'

They were received warmly by Sangye and her parents. It was a quaint and tranquil place with a small stream flowing placidly through their settlement. Sangye served them tea and lunch with Tibetan Cuisine. They were hungry and ate too much of their food. After a rest Sangye took them to the stream which was full of white pebbles. The people in the surrounding areas came to see them and asked a lot of questions. Sangye accompanied them to Namdroling monastery and golden temple, Kushalnagar. She took them around and showed the statues of Buddha, library, colleges etc and then took them to the main hall where pin drop silence prevailed. They sat down along with others and meditated for about 30 mts. After spending about one hour there, they returned to Virajpet.

The cardamom plants have bloomed and it is a beautiful sight to see. Insects ate all the initial blossoms, before they became seed pods. When they blossomed again, high potency pesticide was sprayed to protect the flowers from insects and flies. Zeenath'll roam through the cardamom plants enjoying the aroma of the spice and once they saw vipers sleething in the gap between plants. She was terrified and shrieked in fear the women workers rushed to the spot to help her. By that time, the snakes disappeared into a hole.

The pods become ripe in many stages. The ripe pods are plucked then and there without causing damage to the other pods and collected in sacks. They are carried to the oven for drying. The oven is a big room in which there is a ceiling made of steel net of tiny mesh. Firewood is burned in the floor and the hot air is passed through the ceiling on which plucked pods are spread for drying. After drying, the cardamom pods are removed from the ceiling for classification. They are segregated quality wise and packed in gunny bags for marketing .Green pods are superior and will fetch high price, brown and grey are considered Inferior in quality.

Jahanara and daughters went to meet Chengappa sir and family. At that time, they were celebrating Puthari festival in their house. A lot of people, both men and women had assembled over there, in colourful dress. After sumptuous lunch they began to dance. Chengappa, his wife, daughter and daughter- in- law participated in the dance. There was a music party and one man with a drum. Jahanara and daughters were also invited to participate in the dance by Nina Chengappa. All of them danced according to the rhythm of puthari chathe songs for about half an hour. It was really a delightful experience.and they enjoyed very much in the gaiety.and ecstasy of harvest festival.

After the vacation Rabia and Zeenath returned to their hostel and Jahanara's life became dull and monotonous again. Her main entertainment is Kannada serial. She used to spend hours seeing serials in Suvarna and two other channels. Most of the serials are tragic in nature and Jahanara is very kind hearted and she used to weep seeing the tragic end of some serials.

Once, she saw a serials with her own story and that day she could not sleep and she recalled her old happy and harmonious life, with Rafeeque. Now, she is a divorcee and life is really desperate and dull. She thought for a second about suicide. Then, she corrected herselfand said to herself 'No I'll never commit suicide. I've to live for my children. If they hate me I'll put an end to my worthless life.'

@@@@@@@

11. Maj. Devaiah proves his worth

After taking charge as Factory Manager, Devaiah streamlined the work of the factory and Improved the efficiency and output of the factory. Devaiah visited each and every corner of the factory and store depot and noted that the factory was found in a shabby and littered condition. Loose tea dust were lying at all places and the processed tea was lying in mounds in a hall for days together. The workers did not care to wear cap and gloves while dealing with tea dust. He instructed all staff to wear hygienic caps and gloves while working in factory. His second instruction was to wash the chapp before sending them to the drying chamber. Even though, there are standing instructions to wash the leaves, before processing, these instructions are not followed in most factories. High potency pesticide is sprayed on the tender leaves and the spraying will continue till the date of plucking. So if leaves are processed without proper wash and cleaning pesticide residue will remain in the processed tea. His third instruction was to pack the processed tea in big gunny bags immediately after production and keep them properly in store depot, till they are transported to Chennai, for auction.

The store was cleaned and all unnecessary gunny bags and old stock of tea were removed and destroyed. Also the store was modified to stop the entry of rodents like rats, mice etc. Now the factory got a face lift. The workers were very cooperative with Devaiah and loved him and respected him. He helped them in all respects and started a credit society to reduce their financial woes.

Devaiah was happy at Kotagiri. Now, two years have elapsed, after joining duty at Kotagiri. He had no financial problems since he was getting a handsome amount of pension, every month, in addition to salary. His wife was a graduate and hence he managed to get a job for her in the school, as office clerk. His step-son was very intelligent and shone in his studies. Every month, Devaiah made a visit to the Agrahara jail and met his boss- Rafeeque.

After three years, Rafeeque got a parole for one month and he spent one week in his bungalow, looking after estate matters, reading and sleeping. Devaiah used to meet him daily and discuss various issues.

`Devaiah sir I've a plan to visit Calcutta next week'.

`Is it for sightseeing?' Devaiah enquired.

`No, I want to meet a friend there. She was previously store keeper, here.'

`Oh! Saira Bhanu I didn't post anybody in her place and I myself am managing that job.'

`OK, then you can claim some honorarium for the additional work'

`Rafeeque, I don't have much work here and I find it a pleasure to manage store also. I don't want any additional pay for that.'

`Devaiah sir, do you know more about Calcutta city and its suburbs? I want to make a visit to that historic city? I've lived in Calcutta cantonment for two years. I know most of the places there. It is long past and the face of Calcutta would have changed thoroughly, during the last 30 years.'

`I've visited Calcutta once, when I was free after education. I went up to Sunderbans and spent one week there. This is a different place. Have you heard of Alipore?'

`I've heard about Alipore jail. Our Mahatma Gandhi has spent many years in Alipore jail.'

`OK, I've read about it. This house is in the vicinity of the jail. Saira is living with her mother and brother. She is a relative of our Tipu Sultan. She has completed LLB and got enrolled in the Calcutta bar as junior advocate. She is a wonderful lady and worked as maid in my bungalow, when her husband was lying ill. I didn't know that she was a graduate and law student.'

`What happened to her husband?'

`She married a Christian and had to flee from Calcutta for her life. Finally, they reached Kotagiri and got a job in a tea estate. He was a drunkard and became a liver patient and breathed his last. They have got a daughter named Jessinda.'

` Rafeeque, our Chengappa is in great distress now '.

`What happened to him?'

`His son married a medical student from Bangalore. She is now working as doctor in Mahaveer hospital. Now, it is more than three years after the marriage and he has not made a visit to India to meet her or take her to US. It is heard that he is not sending any letters to her or talk to her over phone. That girl is now in great mental agony and grief. It seems he is having another wife in US. Her father became very angry and made a flight to US and was terrified to see that he had an American wife and one kid, there. She was a nurse in his hospital. Now, they have moved necessary papers for divorce. He may come and present himself in the court for final settlement of the case. Chengu will have to give a huge amount as compensation, for spoiling the life of an innocent girl.'

`Nobody told me about this case. I sympathise with Chengappa sir. He may be ashamed and desperate since he is really a gentleman'.

`There is another news about your wife. Your driver Akbar Khan had committed suicide and a legal and Police fight is going on, saying that it was a murder. Local police closed the case as suicide and then the joint action council met CM and DGP and they have ordered reinvestigation of the case.'

`Why did he commit suicide? He was a good boy and a distant relative of Jahanara.'

For some people, it is a joke to make suicide as murder and take pleasure out of the grief of others. I feel sorry about Jahanara.'

`Your daughters are going to become doctors. Both of them are in third year of MBBS.'

`Allah, I can't believe this news. Since I had no contact with my family for years, I don't get any news from there. Thank you Devaiah sir, for this great news. I want to see them. Get details from Chengappa regarding the college and other details?'

`OK, Rafeeque I'll collect it immediately.

Rafeeque air dashed to Calcutta and met Saira Bhanu. She was in great ecstasy in his arrival. After landing in the airport, he checked into a hotel and went to her house next day and spent six hours in her house. He had taken with him some gifts to Jessinda and the children of her brother. Saira Bhanu prepared many Bengali cuisines and made him eat. During conversation, he asked. ` I want to make you my own. After two years, I'll come out of the jail. If you are with me, it'll transform my life. It'll be a great boon and achievement. I can say with pride that, my wife is a relative of the legendary Sultan. I can never reunite with Jahanara. You work here for two years and then I'll come and take you to Kotagiri. You can do practice at Ooty court, if you want to practice. Otherwise, you can work as legal advisor of our estate and I'll offer you a big package. Now I'm paying huge amount, for legal advice. '

`Rafeeque sir, I can't give you any assurance now. My daughter is growing up and I've to perform my duty as a mother. She has no father.' Saira said in subdued tone

`OK, it is true. I 'm not compelling you. I love you very much with all my heart and would like to make you my life partner, for the rest of my life.' He entreated.

`I want you to reunite with your family. Otherwise, it'll be a curse on my head.'

`How can I approach her for reunion? She is an aggressive lady and not like you or others? Another hassle is that, to take back after triple talaq, she has to marry another man and get divorce. It is not easy as you think. I've no guilty conscience in this regard.'

`We can think over it, later.'

`If you want anything, please tell me.'

`You have given me enough love and money. Some money is still balance in my account. I don't require anything now. I've no words to thank you for your kind visit to my house, at such a distant and unfamiliar place. I never thought that you will visit my house' Saira Bhanu became very sad and emotional and tears welled in her eyes instantly and it streaked down through her cheeks.

She tried to suppress her emotions but failed and it exploded in the form of violent grief.

`Saira, don't cry. Please leave it; don't worry, I'll come again.'

Rafeeque spoke for a long time with her mother and brother in Urdu. Jessinda returned from school at 5 pm and she came to him and made enquiries about his life and also about Kotagiri. By nightfall, Rafeeque returned to his hotel and caught return flight to Coimbatore and reached Kotagiri, in a gloomy state of mind.

After two days, Rafeeque made a trip to the Medical College, Bangalore to meet his daughters. He met them in their hostel and spoke for about one hour. Rafeeque could not recognize them, since they had become tall and fair. Rabia and Zeenath broke into tears on seeing their daddy.

`I thought you will come to meet me in Agrahara jail, but nobody turned up. So, I came to see you. Are you happy and comfortable here?'

`Yes daddy, we are now in third year. It is Chengappa sir who helped us to get admission in the Management quota.'

`How much donation did you pay?'

` I think some forty lakhs for both of us.'

`How did she make such huge money?'

`Bank loan was received '

`Any way, you are lucky to become medical students. I'll come out of the jail, when you pass out as doctors.'

`Do you want anything to drink?' Rabia asked.

`No beti, I don't want anything. It was a long cherished dream to meet you and I 'm fully happy and satisfied now.'

`Daddy, try for reconciliation with Mama. She is very innocent .Our life is gone without you.' Zeenath said in tears.

`Beti, I've no other wife at Kotagiri. That lady was my maid and she has gone back to her house at Calcutta.'

`Then, daddy try for a reunion.'

`I 'm willing, but there are some hurdles. First thing your Mama is very rigid and sentimental She'll never agree for a reunion.'

`Let us try and make her agree for that '. Both of them said in unison.

`Another hurdle is that I had slapped triple talaq on her. To take her back she has to marry another man and get divorce. It appears rather difficult. Anyway, you talk to her and get her consent.'

Rafeeque spent there for about one hour and left. At the time of parting, he enquired` do you require money?'

`No daddy, Mama is giving enough every month. Thank you daddy.'

`You speak to your Mama and settle things. I 'm ready for any agreement that'll restore our family life. Daddy is going.' Rafeeque said goodbye.

 Rafeeque went out of the gate and walked briskly. He caught a cab and went to Shivaji Nagar. He had to enquire at two or three places, to find out the residence of his paternal uncle, Feroz. There was a watchman at the gate and he enquired with him` Feroz is my uncle. Is he inside?

`He is in the office. You can call him through intercom'.

`Please call him, now itself.'

The watchman dialled and handed over the receiver to Rafeeque.'

`Uncle, I'm Rafeeque .I've come to your house and standing at the watchman cabin'.

`Rafeeque, please wait there. I'll be there within ten minutes.'

By the time, he put down the receiver, a luxury car appeared at the gate and one bearded old man with skullcap, got down from the car and approached him, with a smile on his face.

`Oh! It is a miracle. What happened to you to come to this place?'

`Uncle, excuse me. Even though, we are close relatives, we've not met each other for years. I clearly remember you had come for the funeral of daddy. After that, we haven't met each other.'

`That is true. I'd received intimation of your mother's demise, but I was about to go to Haj, at that time. Sorry for not meeting you for such a long time .Then, how are you? How is your family?'

`All are fine'

`Let us go home and talk.'

Rafeeque walked behind him.

Feroz called his wife, daughter- in- law and grandchildren and introduced them to Rafeeque. They stared at him as if they are seeing him, for the first time.

`Be seated Rafeeque. I've not seen your wife and children. You bring them here one day.'

`OK uncle, we can think over it. Where is Mansoor uncle living?'

`He is now in UK. He has a lot of business enterprises here and in UK. The business here was given to his son-in- law and he migrated to UK, with family. He is now a billionaire there.'

`Uncle, where is your office and what is your business here?' Rafeeque enquired.

`I've a five star hotel, a Multi-specialty hospital, one Medical college and one Engineering College.' Feroz said proudly. .

`Do these institutions come under trusts, proprietary concerns or partnership firms?' Rafeeque enquired.

`All are proprietary concerns; but in records they are registered under charitable trusts. What is your business, Rafeeque?'

`I've two coffee estates and one tea estate.'

`Rafeeque, I 'm a bit busy I've an appointment with the Education Minister. You can stay here for a few days. We are meeting after a long time. We can talk the whole night. Salim, show him his room'.

`No uncle, I've to return to Ooty, now itself. I'll come later and then we can talk.'

Rafeeque went out briskly, hired an auto and left.

When he was travelling in the bus to Ooty, he recollected the story of that forest brigand Ponnappan which bapa had told him when he was a student. That Ponnappan is very old now and is hiding somewhere, as a fugitive. Many of his relatives had been hunted and house raided by police and special protection force. Some of his comrades arrested by police had been awarded with death penalty, for offences like conspiracy, murder, plunder, rape etc and killing of elephants in large numbers, cutting of sandalwood trees from forests etc. etc. Those people who became rich through him are living as ideal citizens, in wealth, pomp and luxury and Rafeeque is one among them. Rafeeque felt a kind of guilty feeling and sympathised with that old man who was his daddy's friend and accomplice.

Rafeeque spent the remaining days in reading and watching TV. One morning he heard the call from the mosque. Then, he took his car and rushed to the mosque and prayed to Allah to make his life peaceful. He earnestly regretted the mistakes on his part and begged for redemption.

Every day, Devaiah will visit him in the evening and discuss factory matters. But, he looked gloomy and did not show any interest, in the affairs of estate or factory. As a duty, he heard everything patiently and did not say much.

`Rafeeque, there is a news. Chengappa's son has landed and he signed the joint petition for consensus divorce. He paid an amount of Rs 25 lakhs to his wife, as compensation. Thus, that marriage has ended in failure. That girl had made a suicide attempt and with the grace of god she escaped.'

`Man proposes and god disposes. That is cent percent correct. Things are not in our hands. There is some force in the universe and we call it Allah or God and that power is deciding our fate. We are only pawns in his hand.'

`Yes Rafeeque, you are correct. My sons are still my enemies. They've not made even a call to me. My daughter and son-in-law had visited us once and stayed one night with us.'

`When?'

`You'd gone to Calcutta at that time.'

`I feel a special affinity to your son- in- law. '

`He is a nice boy and loved by one and all.' Devaiah said.

`Where is his mother now? Just convey my enquiries when you meet her '.

`I once told her about you and she could not recollect your name.'

`She was my classmate for BCom and I still remember her face. She stopped her education after degree and did not try for post - graduation. Had she tried, she would have got a job in government service.'

`My daughter has one child and she is looking after that kid now.'

Rafeeque spent the whole day in his bungalow, reading books. He had purchased some new books from Bangalore and enjoyed the pleasure of reading. He relished the book- War and Peace, Anna Karenina Gone with the wind, Mayor of Casterbridge, Sons & Lovers, And Quiet Flows the Dawn, City of Joy and Freedom at Midnight. He had covered all books of Leon Uris and some interesting novels of James Hardy Chase. He had also read some Kannada books by Dr.Ananthamurthy also. By reading world classics and American Literature his perspective about the world has completely changed.

One day, he went to the office of Cherian and spent a lot of time discussing the various problems of the estate.

`Cherian, how much have you paid towards the overdraft?'

`Sir, we have repaid about 30 lakhs and 20 lakhs are outstanding. After the next auction, we can remit some more amount to the loan. Our financial position is positive and I am optimistic of further improvement.'

`OK, good, maintain good relation with the workers.'

`No labour problems in our estate and it gives us much satisfaction'.

`What about Moopanar estate?'

`It is now under receiver rule. The court has appointed a receiver and it is under receiver rule now.'

`OK, who is the receiver?'

`It is an advocate named Pandyan. He is a politician- cum- don and the workers are afraid of him.'

`Cherian, my parole is over and I'll return to the jail tomorrow.'

`OK sir, I'll come and visit you whenever required.'

Rafeeque said goodbye to Devaiah and returned to Bangalore.

@@@@@@@

12.   Jahanara resents reunion

When Rafeeque returned to his cell, his cellmate Abdul Sathar was found sitting with a bandage on his neck.

`Sathar what happened to your neck?' Rafeeque asked.

`Some people tried to kill me in day light, within the jail premises. With the grace of the omipotent and almighty Allah, I escaped.'
He narrated a heart wrenching incident.

`After Rafeeque left on parole, I went out to prune the plants in the garden as ordered by the warden. When I was doing the job, a group of convicts came and hit me in the back and neck. I fell down with the force of the blow and blood flowed from a deep cut near my neck. I got one blow on my head also. I lost my conscience and fell down. By that time, other inmates and jailors came rushing and over-powered them. I was immediately removed to the hospital. There was a deep wound in the neck and one disc in my neck was dislocated and I was in the hospital, for three weeks. The attackers were born criminals and they had been bribed by the relatives of Anwar whom I'd killed. My neck is slightly bent and I've severe pain while turning the neck'.

`Where are the culprits?'

`They are still inside the jail. They are born criminals, undergoing life imprisonment for murder. They are four in number and I've seen them before, many times.'

`Was there any action against them?'

`A criminal case has been registered against them for murder attempt. I've heard that many murder gangs are available in Tihar jail. I never thought that, such gangs are available here also. '

`Yes I've read about the murder of Rajan Pillai, big business magnate who came here as fugitive from Singapore was murdered inside the Tihar jail , by some inmates .They were funded by some businessmen of Mumbai, who had a grudge against Pillai. His wife had lodged a complaint in the court to save his life, but the court did not take it serious. Next day, he was murdered inside the jail premises.'

`This is India. The jail authorities may also get share of the booty, for giving indirect support.'

`Rafeeque, we are not safe in jail also. My wife is laid up after hearing the horrible incident.'

Antony was sitting idle and did not say anything, on hearing about the tragic incident. For three weeks, he was alone in the cell. When Abdul Sathar was brought back from the hospital, he did not ask him anything and sat like a statue. It seemed that he had some mental problem. But, he does not request the jail authorities for medical treatment.

`Sathar, why is he sitting like this? I think he has some serious psychic problem.' Rafeeque said.

`His wife was living in her brother's house and one day she ran away with another lover. He knew about it and this change came over him, after that incident.'

`I 'm planning to tell the warden to send him to a psychiatrist.'

`Such illness can't be cured easily. He'll be alright if he is released from jail and is settled with a normal family life '.

After three months, Devaiah made a visit to the jail and Rafeeque exulted very much. During conversation, he discussed ways and means to persuade Jahanara for a negotiated settlement.

`Devan sir, ask her to marry somebody known to her family and get divorce as early as possible.

I'm prepared to spend any amount for this purpose. In our community, such name sake Nikah and talaq are usual. She is not going to live with anybody. Just sit for the Nikah and that is all.

`It is better to consult a Maulvi for this purpose.'

`I'll speak to Chengappa also in this regard. He has more influence over her.'

`Do as you think more easy and harmless.'

When they were talking Rabia and Zeenath came. They also took part in the conversation.

`Mama is not an ordinary lady and I don't think she'll agree to this proposal. She has already

Suffered a lot recently. She is a bold lady and may prefer to remain alone.' Rabia said.

`Mummy is angry to all of us, for making her life a hell. People are mocking at her for everything.'

Some gossip mongers are spreading scandal stories about her. She is a bold and courageous lady'.

`It is difficult to change her mind.' Zeenath interrupted.

Finally, Rabia and Zeenath agreed to speak to her mother about the reunion and inform

Devan sir, the result of their efforts. He has promised to meet her parents and brothers and discuss this issue with them. After completion of the allotted time, Devaiah left for Kotagiri and daughters to their hostel.

After one week, Rabia and Zeenath visited their home and presented this issue before their Mama, Jahanara.

`Mama, daddy had come to our hostel when he was on parole. After that we made a visit to his jail some time back. He is earnestly   longing to reunite with you.' Zeenath said.

`Oh! He is trying to canvass your support. Why did you go to meet him in the jail? Are you trying to isolate me? I've nobody in this world. I thought you'll be with me, till my death, but you are also with your daddy and I 'm out.'

`No Mama, he has no other wife there. People are spreading scandals due to jealousy. She was only a maid and she has gone back to her home at Calcutta. Don't blame him unnecessarily. By the time, he comes out, we must settle this issue. He has instructed Devan sir to meet uncles and grandpa for their support.' Rabia spoke in a friendly way.

`All are trying to make my life hell. I'll never agree for another marriage and divorce. It is pure nonsense.'

`Grandpa will find out a fellow from Mysore and everything will end amicably. Daddy is ready to spend any amount for this purpose. There was some curse to our family and that is the cause of these problems. It is not correct to blame him alone for what happened.'

`No, I don't want to hear anything. I'll never bend my head before anybody for Nikah; please don't compel me.' Jahanara was very firm and resolute in her conviction.

Devaiah went to Mysore and spoke to Jaleel and Anwar and discussed the issue .He spoke to their parents also.

`Sir, he'd a wife there and I've seen that lady with my own eyes. Now, he would have shifted her to some other place. The workers told me that he was staying with her in the new house Purchased by him for 18 lakhs. They also told me about his frequent visits to Paradise hotel for revelry with wives of businessmen and officers. He is a real cheat and I can't believe him'

`I'm living in that house, where she and her daughter were staying. She's gone back to Calcutta.'

`First we have to see whether sister is willing for reunion. If she resents reunion with him, it is waste of time and energy.' Jaleel said.

Jaleel offered to visit her and ascertain her views.

Devaiah went back to Kotagiri and informed Rafeeque about his visit to Mysore, when he visited him in jail, after one week.

After a few days, Jaleel and Anwar visited Jahanara. She was in full spirits and discussed with them her views about reunion.

`Didi, Rafeeque had sent a messenger to our house. He is badly in need of reunion. He is about to be released from prison. That lady has gone back to Calcutta and he can't live without a wife.'

`Jaleel, my daughters had presented this subject to me when they came last time. They are anxious because a daddy is necessary for conducting their marriages. They'll become doctors after one year. But, I'm against a reunion. That is not because, I hate him after the stabbing incident. I've to marry another person and spend one night with him and then get divorce and then Nikah with Rafeeque. It is better to remain single for the rest of my life. This is my decision. You can convey the same to him.'

Jaleel tried many coaxing and cajoling and still she remained adamant in her conviction.

`If it is your decision, we have nothing to say.'

They returned to Mysore in the evening.

After two months, Rabia and Zeenath visited Jahanara and again sought the opinion of their mother, in reunion. Then Jahanara became violent and fired her daughters.

`If you love your daddy go and live with him. I told you my opinion that I don't want to bend my head before anybody .Gone is gone and I've no regrets. How can I live with a husband who tried to kill me? How can I live with a husband who was unfaithful to me? There may be ladies who are unable to respond and ready to suffer any ignominy and harassment from the husbands. I don't want any companion for the rest of my life. Don't try to compel me to do anything which I don't like.'

After saying this, Jahanara broke into tears; walked to her room and fell on the bed. Rabia and Zeenath became very much worried and tried to console their mother.

`Maa, we'll never compel you in future. Please excuse me this time. I'll not repeat it in future.' Rabia entreated in tears.

`Mama please excuse me for causing irritation to you. I'll never repeat this in future.' Zeenath begged.

Rabia and Zeenath met their daddy and informed him about the strong objection from their mother for reunion.

`If she is not interested, I don't take more interest, in this case. Don't compel her if she is against reunion.'

`OK, daddy. We won't say anything in this regard.'

After a couple of months, Jaleel came to meet Jahanara.

`Didi, recently I met a businessman in Mysore, who stopped his business owing to heavy loss. He is urgently in need of one lakh; otherwise he'll have to vacate his shop room. He is willing to marry you and divorce, for the reunion. There is no compulsion that you should live with him one day. If we pay him one lakh, the problem is solved.' Jaleel advised.

`But, Jaleel, religious rules are rules and it can't be broken. So, I won't agree to this suggestion'. Jahanara was very firm in her conviction.

Jaleel returned to Mysore in disappointment.

After one month, Mohsin came for a casual visit of the cardamom plantation. He appreciated Jahanara in her great success, in the cardamom farming.

`Jahanara, I'm very much impressed in the high profit obtained this year. If you want, you can expand this farming to more areas here and Hassan.'

`No, Mohsin I 'm in great tension and worry. My children and brothers are compelling me for reunion with my husband. It is not an easy thing. I thought over it many times and discarded the idea. How can I marry a person, live with him for few days and get divorce? It is not at all possible. I hate that proposal and I can't bend my head for that. If we are united it'll be a boon for my daughters. We've to conduct their marriage without delay and our living separate will be a problem for my daughters marriage.'

`I can understand your worries and mental conflicts. If you want I'm ready to help you. I'll never insist you to live with me.'

`Thank you, Mohsin. It'll be a great sacrifice on your part, but I can't bring myself to agree to it.'

`How can I live with a husband who cheated me and tried to kill me? I can't forget it. It is better to live separate till death.'

Mohsin was really surprised in the grit and determination of a simple village maiden, like Jahanara. Her unflinching courage and fortitude to live alone, the entire life really baffled him,

Much water flowed through Cauvery river and Rabia and Zeenath completed their course and Passed in first class. The house surgeoncy was also completed and both of them joined the same institution, as tutors. They wanted to join for MD, but Jahanara objected. You make money by working and take post - graduation later on. A major portion of your loan is still pending.' Jahanara said.

Some marriage proposals came for Rabia , but Jahanara turned them down .

One case came from Silk Board, Bangalore. The boy is a doctor in government service. His father was an officer in the Industries department and they belonged to Mangalore.

`Let her stand on her own feet and then we'll think over marriage.' Jahanara told them.

`Madam, we don't compel you to conduct it now. You decide the case and we are ready to wait.'

`It is not proper to delay inordinately. You find out some other girl.'

After some time, another case came and both the boys are engineers in software companies. They demanded both of them to the same house. This also was turned down saying that it is not proper and auspicious to marry both the girls to the same house.

One day Rafeeque was released from jail without any advance notice. There was some more months for release and he got a reprieve of few months' concession and was released. After coming out of the jail, Rafeeque made a call to his daughter Rabia and informed her the good news. Rabia and Zeenath became jubilant.

'Daddy where will you go?' Zeenath asked.

'I'll go back to Kotagiri .What else can I do?'

'Daddy go and meet Chengappa sir and wife. If they try, Mama may agree.'

'Is it so. Then, I'll go and meet Chengappa sir, now itself.'

Rafeeque went direct to Virajpet and met Chengappa. After bath and sleep, he came down from his room and faced Chengappa.

'Jahanara is adamant for reunion. If you try, she may agree. She respects you more than others.'

'Rafeeque, both of us will make a visit and persuade her for the reunion.'

Chengappa called Nina and said 'Nina, we have to visit Jahanara now itself and convey the good news that Rafeeque has been released from jail. Also we can press her for a reunion with Rafeeque.'

`OK, I'm ready. If we can reunite them, it is a great thing.'

`Rafeeque we'll visit her, in the evening. You stay here for one day'.

`No sir, you try your best and if you succeed, please let me know. I'm leaving for Kotagiri, now itself.'

`OK, Rafeeque we'll let you know, the developments.'

Chengappa and Nina visited Jahanara, that evening and talked with her for two hours and returned home in despair. Jahanara did not agree for any kind of compromise.

`Jahanara, Rafeeque has been released from jail and he is eager to reunite with you. He has repented for what has happened. He is ready even to apologise to you. He has no other wife at Kotagiri. There was a lady and it was his maid and she has returned to her house at Calcutta. Your daughters have become doctors and they have to be given in marriage .If you are living In two different places, their lives will be in jeopardy. For family life, we have to maintain a give and take policy. Without patience, and tolerance family life is not possible. 'Chengappa made an introductory remarks.

`Sir, I've great respect towards you. It is you who helped me for the admission of my daughters.

We had no contact with our close relatives in Bangalore. One of them has a medical college. Relatives are of no use and friends and neighbours are more helpful, now-a-days. We are thankful to you for your invaluable help and advice in my daughter's case. With all respects, I'm saying, I can't reunite with that man. He is a cheat and I don't trust him. From my experience , I can say that living alone is better and I don't want any male as companion, for the remaining part of my life. For this purpose, I abhor to bend my head before a stranger and live with him for few days and get divorce. Prophet was very kind towards women and he decided to punish the erring husbands. If they did anything like this, he should repent the entire life. Let him suffer, if he has done anything wrong. I've already decided to live alone for the rest of my life. Sir, I thank you and Ninadidi for the friendly visit and advice.' Jahanara revealed her mind.

`Jahanara, we've nothing more to say. You are a wise and learned lady and you can take your own decisions .OK, Jahanara, we are leaving.' Chengappa said.

`Jahanara, your decision is correct and I support it. Most of the husbands are selfish. They are concerned about their comforts and pleasure. They are least bothered about the desires and aspirations of their wives. ' Nina Chengappa said.

`Nina, am I like that?'

`No, you are an exception and is very faithful to your wife. I've no complaints about you. Many ladies are really frustrated but they are unable to express it, since they are not self-reliant. If they are self-dependent they can fight with their husbands. If they are helpless and have no option but to suffer the neglect and ill -treatment of their husbands and ill- laws, till death. Employed ladies are very bold and hence domestic quarrels and divorces are high in such families.' Nina blurted out.

`How is your cardamom crop, Jahanara? Is there any profit in it?'

`There is some profit and not much. Initial investment was heavy and it'll take years to make up the investment. Only thing is that we got a long term loan, with nominal interest, for development of the fallow land. It is a labour oriented crop. Too many man hours are required for plucking pods, drying and marketing. Frequent spraying of pesticide is necessary and the cost of pesticide and labour will amount to a good sum, every month. If the price is high, then it is profitable; otherwise we will end up in loss.'

`Many people advised me to cultivate vanilla, but I declined. We can't ensure a good price for this item I've planted pepper at the foot of all shade trees and it is found to be very profitable. Only thing is that labour cost for plucking is very high.' Chengappa said.

After tea and a visit to the cardamom field, Chengappa and wife returned to their house. After reaching there, he dialled Rafeeque and informed him that Jahanara's reply was negative.

That weekend Jaleel and Nazar came to meet Jahanara and spent half a day, in that house.

`Didi, a proposal has come for Rabia, a few days ago. The boy is working in Qatar, as Engineer and his name is Mohammed Saheer. He'll take the girl there after marriage and arrange a job in any of the hospitals, there. They are from Mandya and have enough landed properties. If it is agreeable to you, the marriage can be conducted within two months. The boy is coming on leave shortly.'

'If it is a good case, we can take it. I'm sure that the boy will like our Rabia. We can conduct the marriage of the elder first and wait some more time for the younger.'

'That is better .We can't arrange both the cases together. Some people say it is un-auspicious to conduct both marriages, on the same day.'

'If we will get grooms for both of them, it can be done, on the same day. Otherwise, Zeenath will feel bad. After Rabia's marriage Zeenath will become lonely and feel annoyed.'

'I know this party and don't miss it. We can find out a groom for Zeenath also without delay.'

'Then ask Rabia to come next Sunday and I'll come with them.'

'OK, I'll ask them to come. But, I fear whether they will ask anything about Rafeeque.'

'Didi, don't give full details and simply say that he is at Kotagiri. After the marriage we can tell the full story. If he wanted to see the boy, let him go and meet him '

'If we give those full details, sometimes we will miss the case due to some unseen hurdles.'

'If there is any problem. I'll contact Devan sir and get his consent.'

'OK, that is a good idea.'

'Don't give any publicity. We can inform others after the final confirmation.'

`OK, I won't tell anybody.'

Jaleel and Nazar returned to Mysore after nightfall.

When her brothers left, Jahanara became anxious about her marital status and spent that night haunted by unwanted and awful dreams. Jahanara informed her daughters about the proposal and asked them to come on Saturday. Jaleel came with the party on Sunday morning. The boy was tall and fair with a mole on his left cheek. He was accompanied by his sister and mother. They asked a lot of questions about father, job, income, accommodation and higher studies. Rabia replied to all their questions and enquiries in a pleasing manner and they liked her. Zeenath stood behind her to give support and confidence. After one hour, they returned to their house with Jaleel. At 8 pm Jaleel called Jahanara and said that they liked Rabia and wanted marriage within 10 days, so that the groom can spend here, one month after marriage.

`Jaleel, you please contact Devan sir, give their address and ask him to go there with Rafeeque , meet the groom and settle the case, if he liked the case.'

`OK didi, I'll contact him now itself.'

Devaiah and Rafeeque went to Mandya, the next day and met the groom. Both of them liked the boy, his parents and the house and fixed the marriage, on a Sunday after one week. Immediately, this information was passed on to Jaleel and Jaleel in turn informed Jahanara. Rafeeque had conveyed that the full expenditure of the marriage will be met by him and no need of worry. Jahanara booked an auditorium in the town and started inviting relatives, friends and workers. Only limited people were invited for the marriage in view of the lack of time.

Two days before the marriage, Rafeeque went to Bangalore, took Rabia and Zeenath to a famous jewellery shop and purchased necessary jewellery and took them to Virajpet .On the way they stopped at Mysore and purchased some dresses for them, Jahanara, relatives and maids.

It was dark when they reached their home.

`Daddy has to attend some urgent works and I'm going back now itself' Rafeeque said.

They did not allow him to go back. Both of them pulled his hand and said. `Daddy stay here today and you can go back, tomorrow morning, if you are so busy.'

They went inside and told Jahanara about the arrival of daddy, but she did not come out of the kitchen.

That day, he stayed there in a separate room without being seen by Jahanara. Dinner was served to him by Fatima and Beevi. While returning to Kotagiri he gave a cover to Rabia.

`Rabia, please give this amount to your Mama. This contains two lakhs rupees. I'll come for the marriage, in the early morning, tomorrow.'

The marriage was conducted in an auditorium at Virajpet and all friends and relatives were present. The Nikah was arranged in the early morning, in presence of Rafeeque, groom's father, and the local Maulvi and then the couple were taken to the auditorium, for reception. It was a simple function and there were no pomp, luxury or splurge

After the marriage, Rabia was taken to the groom's house. Rafeeque and Devaiah returned to Kotagiri in the evening. Chengappa and wife were available for the marriage. Many doctors and students had come from the college.

After the marriage, Zeenath stayed with Jahanara for two days and returned to the hospital. Since she became lonely, she had some stress and tension on her face.

`Zeenath, within a short time your marriage also will take place. We are doing everything for the same. Jaleel and Nazar will bring suitable match for you. Don't forget to call me after reaching there.'

Zeenath embraced mama and wept profusely.

`Don't cry beti, our Rabia has escaped and you also will go like that. Don't worry'

`I've no worry Mama. I feel sorry, when I realize that I 'm alone.'

`Her husband will go after one month and she'll be here for six months. She has to apply for passport and it'll take minimum 3 months. Passport particulars have to be given to him and she has to wait till the visa is ready. Then only she can go. Anyway she'll be with you, for six months.'

`I can't believe this news. If it is true I am very happy. I thought she will go to the gulf with her husband immediately leaving me alone.   '
Zeenath wiped her tears and smiled at Mama. `Before she goes

to gulf, your marriage will be conducted. It is almost certain. If anybody comes to see you, I'll inform you and then you should come without fail.'

`OK Mama, I'm going.'

Rabia took one month leave. The couple stayed in Jahanara's house, for one week and then they went to Kotagiri and spent their two days. They also went on a honeymoon trip to Simla. After one month, Mohammed Saheer returned to his work place in Qatar. In the meanwhile, he had made Rabia apply for her passport. Rabia returned to Bangalore after the expiry of one month leave.

Rabia got passport after three months. Within fifteen days, she got visa also. She resigned from the job and flew to Doha alone. Zeenath was in tears for one week. Gradually, she mustered enough courage to face any situation. During the weekend, she came to Virajpet and spent two days with Mama. During conversation, Jahanara told her about a proposal from Hyderabad .The boy is a doctor working in Ranchi. His father was an employee of the Rourkela Steel Plant. After retirement his parents returned to their ancestral house at Hyderabad. The boy continued his study at Ranchi and after MBBS, got a job in the government hospital, there. If you go there, you are also likely to get a job, there.'

`Mama, I'm not interested to work at such places. If there is any case from Bangalore, I 'm willing to accept the same now.'

`Your daddy's uncle Feroz is a big shot there. We've no connection with them for quite a long time. He is having a

Medical college and a hospital there. Had we known about it earlier, you could have been admitted there?'

'These people will never take relatives, because they would have to give some concession, in the donation amount. Unknown people are better than these so called relatives.' Zeenath remarked.

'I 'm too much worried about you. If you are also given in marriage to somebody, my tension is over.'

'Mama, your tension and worry is not going to cease, in the near future. After marriage, you have to attend their delivery, rearing of grandchildren, babysitting etc. Mama, in this world nobody is indispensable. Mama, there is no meaning in worrying unnecessarily. I've seen kids living in orphanages. There is no body to worry for them. Some people throw their babies to the streets and they finally reach orphanages. Some of them are adopted by some childless couples and others live there till their death without getting mother's love and care.'

'A mother is a mother and if I'm not there, you'll feel the difference. Really speaking, I'd thought of committing suicide, when your daddy slapped triple talaq on me and the only reason I refrained from that decision was you, my daughters. I feared that you'll suffer in my absence.' Jahanara began to weep.

'Don't cry Mama, don't cry. I know that you have great love towards us. I won't make any problem to make you worry or cry.' Zeenath hugged Mama and began to cry loudly.

Rabia started sending letters occasionally and also made phone calls. She is happy and wrote a letter. 'Mama, our residence is beautiful and air -conditioned. We have some close friends, from Mysore. Mohammed Saheer had met a Malayali doctor running a chain of hospitals, in gulf countries and he has offered to give me a job. I'll ring you up when the offer letter is received.' Jahanara was overwhelmed with joy, but there was nobody to share it. Then, she dialled her Umma, but she did not hear what she said. She had some hearing problems and no action was taken by Jaleel to rectify it.

One day Zeenath called and said `Mama, there is a doctor here, by name Salim. He is from Laccadive (Laksha -dweep). He is a nice boy and is very fond of me. What shall I tell him?'

`Zeenath, I don't like to send you to Laksha –dweep, even if he is a prince; I can't accept that proposal. Zeenath put down the receiver on hearing Mama's reply.

A good proposal came from, Bangalore city. The boy is an IT professional in a Multinational company and father is a big businessman on MG Road. Zeenath liked the boy and the engagement was conducted on a grand scale. Rabia and Mohammed Saheer could not attend the function and they promised that they would attend the marriage. A probable date was also decided, after a period of three months. After one month, they informed Rafeeque that they are withdrawing from the case. They did not mention any specific reason for the rejection.

`Why did you give your word and agree to the engagement. It is a disgrace to our family. Please tell me the reason for the rejection or I'll approach the court.' Rafeeque became furious.

`We don't like to take a girl from a broken family. We'd engaged a private detective to investigate your case and according to his report, you are a convict and is living as divorcee.' He shot back impolitely.

It was a bolt from the blue and Rafeeque was completely broken down, in the indecent reply. He did not argue with him nor demand compensation, for breaking the agreement. He entrusted Devaiah to inform the news to Jaleel and Jahanara.

Jahanara wept incessantly for one weeks, in the abrupt cancellation of marriage. Zeenath did not show any palpable worry and tension on her face and moved with a bold and resolute mind. When she came to the house during week end, Jahanara hugged her and lamented.

`If they don't like me or my family, let them find out another lady. There is no dearth of ladies and men in this world.'

Another proposal came from Vijayanagara and the boy is a businessman in Bangalore city. They visited Virajpet house, many times, met Rafeeque at Kotagiri and the date for engagement was fixed.

Jahanara hired an auditorium and invited most of her relatives and friends. Two days before the proposed engagement, they withdrew from the marriage. Jahanara had a tough time to inform the guests about the cancellation of the function. They did not specify the reason for the withdrawal. Jahanara guessed that the broken family may be the reason or conviction of Rafeeque. They can't say anything adverse about Zeenath, because she is such a lovely girl in looks and character.

Next weekend, Zeenath came to meet Mama. She looked very cheerful and happy. She hugged Mama and said `Mama, I 'm very bold. These rejections do not touch my mind. I'm thinking of remaining unmarried till death. Marriage is not a must or inevitable for a woman. Even without marriage and kids, she can live her life successfully. I'll show the world that nothing will happen, if I remained unmarried till death, ha, ha, ha, ha............' She laughed as an insane person and Jahanara was terrified on seeing the grimace on her face and her frightening laughter.

`Beti, don't take it seriously. You've enough time to marry .You are still young. Don't laugh like this? I'm unable to bear it .I'm worried that something very bad is going to happen. I'm terribly afraid; I 'm very much scared. I feel a kind of chest pain, I feel excruciating pain, Allah, help me, I'm unable to bear it, Allah save.....' Jahanara pressed her chest and fainted.

Zeenath examined Mama and was terrified. She had no pulse and was breathing heavily. She called Sebastian and took her to hospital, immediately.

On the way she became conscious for a minute; she opened her eyes partly and looked at Zeenath with anxiety and fear. She mumbled something in a semiconscious state. She was admitted in the hospital, but they could not do anything. The doctors tried to revive her heart, but failed. She breathed her last.

` Sorry madam, she had a massive attack'. The doctor told Zeenath.

Zeenath made a loud scream, on hearing the news. She sat on the floor and lamented and slapped on her head and chest .She could not believe that her mother is dead.

Sebastian ran out in grief and informed all concerned.

Jaleel and Nazer arrived there within one hour and arranged to take the body to their residence.

The funeral was arranged on the next day.

Rafeeque and Devaiah reached within two hours.

Rabia and husband reached the following day. Thus Jahanara Begum of Virajpet said goodbye to this world.

@@@@@@@

13. Untimely demise of Zeenath

The sudden demise of Jahanara, completely shattered Zeenath. She did not speak to anybody for two days and showed some signs of psychic disorder. Rafeeque remained at home throughout and took her to a hospital at Mysore. The psychiatrist prescribed some medicines and advised her to take it, regularly for six months.

`You must be careful for some time. Don't break the medicines for six months. If you find relief after six months, you can stop it temporarily; but keep the medicine always with you. Try to avoid stress and strain and unnecessary worries. If you feel uneasiness, you should take one tablet at bedtime.'

Rabia was also grief-stricken but now, she is completely normal and she tried her best to console Zeenath. After one week, Rabia and husband returned to Qatar. Rafeeque stayed there for one month .He had entrusted everything to Cherian and Devaiah and there is nothing to worry about Kotagiri estate. After Jahanara's demise, the two estates became orphan. Rafeeque entrusted the supervisors to look after the estates and he spent the whole day and night inside his house. He really repented for the wrongs done to Jahanara and prayed to Allah for redemption. After one month, Zeenath almost came round to normalcy. Then, she wanted to return to Bangalore and Rafeeque accompanied her to the hospital and from there he went to Kotagiri.

A Manager was appointed at Golden Valley Estate - one Jayasankar from Madikeri and the outhouse was given to him as office- cum- residence. Rafeeque used to come and monitor the functioning of the estates every week. Jayasankar was working in Assam Brook estate, Dibrugarh and took voluntary retirement, after 20 years of service. It was very difficult to work there, as Manager, due to militancy.

`Jaisankar, why did you take voluntary retirement in such a young age?' Rafeeque asked.

`Sir, the Assamese dislike Bengalis and also people from other states. It is a beautiful place, but that beauty is deceptive. Death is lurking everywhere and we can't trust anybody. Once I was abducted from my quarters, by a group of militants and demanded a ransom of Rupees two crores. The company people did not succumb to their demands, even though they threatened that I would be killed. They lodged a police complaint and waited patiently. Somehow, the police found out their hiding place and raided it, in the dead of the night. Two extremists were killed and I was rescued. It was really a miraculous escape. They used me as shield when the firing started and I got one bullet injury, in my shoulder. When the two militants were killed, they abandoned me and fled under the cover of darkness. I lay down on the floor bleeding and was rescued, after the operation was over. I was shifted to the hospital and was discharged after one week. Then, I decided to leave Dibrugarh immediately and submitted papers for voluntary retirement.'

`I've read about Dum Duma estate, which had paid huge amount of ransom, on many occasions. When they approached the government, they were given permission to employ ex - servicemen as security. Now, militancy has come down and peace returned to Assam.'

`But, we can't trust the present lull or respite. All are for money and loot the private as well as Government organizations. My escape was really miraculous.'

`Was your family with you at that time?'

`No, they were taken to Dibrugarh, during the school vacation, some years back and brought them back safely, after two months. They are living in my house at Madikeri and wife is working in a school, there.'

`OK, Jaisankar, you have nothing to worry here, since this is your native place. Even though you are specialised in tea industry, you can look after coffee plantations also. Before joining tea estate, I was working in a coffee estate.'

`Then, no problem; go ahead with confidence. I'll visit once in a blue moon. You are authorised to take all decisions and no need of waiting for my orders.'

`Thank you, sir.'

`Best wishes, go ahead and you will have all supports from me.'

Zeenath used to call Rafeeque every week and informed that she was happy in her work.

`Beti, you can come and stay with me, occasionally. Are you OK now? Was there any problem after you left for Bangalore? Are you taking medicines regularly?' Rafeeque enquired.

`No daddy, I 'm alright. There is heavy work here and no time to think or worry. I've not stopped medicines 'She said.

`Work hard and become a good doctor.'

`I want to go for MD '

` Beti, wait for some more time. We can try for it, next year.'

`Thank you daddy.'

Much water has flowed through Cauvery River and Karnataka and Tamil Nadu continued their fight for the share of this water. One year elapsed after the demise of Jahanara. Zeenath still remembered her beloved mother and shed some drops of tears. Rabia has completely changed and almost forgot her mother, but called daddy, occasionally. She is now a doctor in a famous hospital run by Dr. Azad Thangal. She and her husband decided to remain childless for three years.

Zeenath is now working in OP section. On a Friday, there was no rush at the OP counter and then one man came and sat on the chair in front of her.

`Doctor Madam, I've severe mental pain. Can you give me some medicines?' The stranger requested.

She looked at the stranger, but could not recognize him. He had a cap on his head and forehead and eyes were not clearly visible. She looked again and said faintly.

` Dr. Salim, why do you play with me? Where were you for the last one year?'

`Zeenath, I'd gone to take a diploma, in Orthopaedics in Ramaiah Medical college. The course was completed and I've re-joined duty. Then, how are you? I heard that your mother had passed away. What happened to her? '

`Salim, she had a massive attack and she died instantly'.

`I could not come to your house, deep condolences'

`Thank you for the belated condolences. Salim, how is your dweep now? Are you in the habit of visiting your parents?'

`How can I forget my home and my dear and near. I'd visited dweep six months back. Do you want to see our paradise .It is now a tourist hub? So many resorts have sprung up and there is heavy flow of tourists to see that archipelago.'

`How many dweeps(islands) are there?

`Mainly four islands and there are more than 36 atolls, most of which are uninhabited. It is a wonderful sight to see these atolls. If you are really interested, come with me.'

`We can arrange a trip.'

`What about your marriage?'

`I 'm ready, but nobody is prepared to marry me.'

`Don't worry, I'm prepared. Are you willing to marry me? Mainland ladies have an aversion to Islanders. You are also one among them. One year back, I'd proposed and you turned down my offer, saying that your Mama was not willing to send you to the dweep. Have you changed your mind now?'

`All Mamas are like that. They want to see their daughters, frequently. We can't find fault with them. It is their selfishness. Now, my Mama is in heaven and I can decide my likes and dislikes.'

`Then OK, I 'm hundred times willing to marry you. You'll definitely like our place. It is 100% Muslim populated area. We are Malayalees migrated from Kannur. These islands were under the rule of Kolathiri Rajas of Kannur. Later, they gifted these islands to Arakkal Royal family, which was the only Muslim kingdom in Kerala. Then, Britishers came and they liked these islands very much. The present Administrator set up was done by them. This place is still ruled by an Administrator. They are more efficient and helpful to the people than elected government. We've no complaints in the present set up. There is one MP from this place. What more do you want to know.' Salim asked smiling.

`OK, I'll speak to my daddy. He is a very friendly person. You bring your parents here and we can arrange the marriage here and then go to the dweep. Are you OK?'

`OK'

Zeenath spoke to her daddy and he agreed without any objections. Next day, itself he came to Bangalore and met Salim and gave his final consent.

`I've spoken to my parents and they are also agreeable. They say that the marriage can be conducted there. So all of us have to go there'

`OK, you make the arrangements and I'll meet all the expenses.'

After one week, all of them went to Cochin and stayed in a hotel. The party included Jaleel, Nazar, Devaiah and a few friends from the hospital. Next day, they boarded the ship to Kavaratti the weather was very fine and hence journey was very pleasant. It took six hours to reach Kavaratti. After anchoring of the ship, they were asked to climb down to the boats stationed below. Some people were very afraid while descending to the boats since the boats were rocking.

They were accommodated in a luxury hotel and Salim went home to make arrangements for the marriage. After two days, the marriage was arranged at the house of Salim. For Nikah, the main Khazi of the island was also present. There was big feast in connection with the marriage, in which hundreds of people participated.

After the marriage, Rafeeque and others visited the other three islands namely Minicoy, Agatti, and Kadamat. They witnessed scuba diving and visited some lagoons and coral reefs. The sight of uninhabited atolls was very thrilling. Small pieces of land lay scattered in the sea with full of vegetation and coconut palms. Salim had taken permission from the office of the Administrator for visiting these atolls.

Zeenath and Salim were ecstatic after marriage and they visited Rafeeque and guests at the hotel, daily. When the return journey date approached, Zeenath became emotional and began to cry. Rafeeque consoled her, in every way, possible.

`Don't cry, be cheerful. This is a beautiful place and we'll come here, occasionally'.

`I know you are saying this to console me'.

`When are you returning to Bangalore?'

`We've taken one month leave. We've a plan to visit important places in Kerala also like Munnar, Alappuzha etc.'

`OK, you take your own time and enjoy honeymoon.'

They said goodbye and left for Kotagiri.

Two weeks passed after return from Kavaratti. During this period, Zeenath had called twice. From her conversation he realized that she is moody and not well.

`Beti, how is life there? What about Salim and your in- laws?'

`Daddy, I'm not well. The climate is horrible here and there is heavy wind blowing from the sea. It has a salty taste. We can see the sea from here. I saw many big ships passing through this route. I feel bored seeing water, boats, fishermen, coconuts and fishing nets, everywhere.'

`When are you going to Munnar and Alappuzha?'

`We've dropped that plan. I 'm worried and homesick. One day, I saw my mother in a dream and she was crying. From that day onwards, I'm taking that medicine- phenobarbitone. It is sleeping pills.' Before completing these lines she broke into tears.

`If you are bored of the island life, please return to Bangalore, at the earliest.'

`But, Salim has some engagements. He is going to buy a property here.'

`Don't worry beti, be cheerful and happy. You are alright.'

It was a Sunday and Rafeeque got a phone call from Salim. He was sobbing while talking.

`Daddy, Zeenath is in hospital. Yesterday she took more sleeping pills. Today, she did not wake up and then she was taken to hospital immediately. The doctor said that she had taken more sleeping pills.'

`How is she now?'

`She is still unconscious and her condition is very serious.'

`Salim, don't worry. I'm starting immediately.'

After one hour another call was received.

`Daddy, she has gone.' Salim broke into tears.

Rafeeque was shocked and he broke down, hearing the news. He could not control his grief and slumped into the sofa and wept.

Rafeeque and Devaiah started to Kavaratti, immediately and reached there next day. They were waiting for their arrival to start the funeral ceremony.

`Do you want to take her body to mainland?' Salim asked Rafeeque in grief stricken voice.

`No, Salim, this is her house and we can bury her, here.'

A large crowd had gathered there hearing the news of the demise of the lady doctor. They accompanied the bier to the burial ground along with many others. The sky was overcast and it started drizzling. That night Rafeeque and Devaiah spent in their house and next day they returned to Kotagiri.

Rafeeque was depressed and dejected after the demise of Zeenath. One day, he went to Virajpet and Kushalnagar with a cap on his head. After a lot of enquiry, he found out the house of Adv. Ashik. Krithika only was available in the house and she invited him to the sit out. Krithika had become an old woman, with full of grey strands in her hair, She wore a shabby saree and the face looked weak and sickly.

`I 'm coming from Kotagiri. Where is Ashik? '

`He has gone to the court. Who are you?'

`I 'm Rafeeque. Do you remember me? I came here to express my regret for spoiling your life and beg pardon for my wrongs. My bapa was a wicked man and he ill -treated your father. Please excuse me, for all the mistakes and sins committed by me and my father,'

Krithika was startled and her face became sad and crestfallen.

`What is the use of this regret, in the evening of my life? It is I who sent my father to beg before your father. He was driven out by your father. I've no feeling of vengeance against you. You are very rich and influential, but I was the daughter of a poor farmer. I lived a life of agony and misery.' Krithika sobbed.

`Krithika, is Ashik my son?'

`No, his father is Bopanna. '

`One of my friends told me that you were pregnant at the time of marriage. You told the truth to your husband and he condoned your mistake and loved you till his death. Is it true?'

`My son is an advocate and I don't want to ruin his life and career. If the truth comes out, his life will be spoiled. Hence, I'll never reveal the truth'.

`Don't punish me or ill-treat me for my mistakes. I've repented a hundred times for that wrongs. Devaiah is with me in my estate. I want to sell that estate. If you can afford it, you take it for a nominal sum. I know you can't take it alone, it is worth crores of rupees. Without giving anything, I'm going to give that estate to our son. Our son will get major share in my estate. If I give it free, it will raise many questions. So, I'll include Devaiah also, in this deal. I'm fed up of life and is relocating to Bangalore, to spend the remaining part of my life. My wife passed away one year back and now my second daughter also met with the same fate. I want to go to Bangalore and spend the rest of my life, in prayers and charity. Before that, I want to do some justice to my son.'

` We don't want anything from you. Please don't make our life miserable.'

`Never, I've been carrying this secret in my mind for years. I'd come for the marriage of Ashik and avoided meeting you. I've met Ashik and his wife, several times. Devaiah sir, is my close friend. You can believe and trust me fully in this regard.'

`He is your son. I was pregnant at the time of marriage. My husband was a great man and he pardoned me. It is I who brought up his sons. They are now in high positions.'

'This is enough for me. My mind has become light with the revelation of the truth by you. My mind has been tormenting me for years. I can't give the entire wealth to my daughter. My son also deserves it. I'll do what is just and legitimate, after due consideration of all aspects. Initially, it 'll be given on lease and later the same will be transferred to the name of Ashik, his wife and Devaiah sir and I won't accept more than 1 crore. Devaiah sir can afford that amount.'

'Don't share this secret with anybody else, especially Devaiah.'

'Never, it will remain a secret, till my death.'

' I'll never disclose this to anybody. I 'm a happy man now. This is a part of nirvana or redemption from my sins. He can continue his profession here or come and work there, as legal advisor of the company. My bungalow is there and he and his family can stay there. He will get his share of my property. If he wants to continue here, let him continue here and come and monitor the functioning of the estate, occasionally.

'I never thought you'll come to see me. Rafeeque, I've suffered a lot because of my son. Now, his father has come in search of him. I'm the happiest woman in the world.'

Rafeeque took her hands in his and kissed it when some drops of tears fell into her palms and he said goodbye.

@@@@@@@

14. Epilogue

One year passed after the death of Zeenath. Now Rafeeque is a sad and reclusive man. He rarely talks to anybody. Devaiah comes to his bungalow and spends about one hour with him .The estate is running on good profit and still he has no interest in its affairs. After the demise of Zeenath, he has visited Virajpet only twice.

Rabia and husband came and stayed with Rafeeque for one week and went back to Qatar. They invited him to Doha for a change of environment, but he refused. One day, he got a letter from Saira Bhanu. She did not know anything about the tragic incidents, in his life. He did not inform her, about the demise of Jahanara and Zeenath.

Dear Rafeeque sir,

Nothing is known about you for a long time. I hope you are keeping good health. Last day I had a dream in which I saw you in a depressed state; your face looked grim and morose and you had a long beard also.

My daughter has been married to a distant relative of mine. He is in government service. My daughter was poor in studies and she did not complete her higher secondary. Freddy's relatives did not show any interest in her. Hence, she was taught Islamic lessons and given in marriage to Mr. Abdul Rizwan who is working as Section Officer, in the Writers building. He is a good boy and will look after my daughter well. My practice is very poor. I 'm still a junior advocate and the income Is hardly sufficient for my day to day life. If there is vacancy of legal officer in your estate, I am willing to come over there.

With regards, Saira Bhanu.

Rafeeque immediately sent a reply stating that there is no vacancy at present and he is planning to dispose of the estate for relocating   to Bangalore, for spending the evening of his life

Rafeeque called Devaiah and Cherian to his bungalow.

`Cherian, have you paid off the balance in the overdraft?'

`Yes sir, now there is no liability for our estate.'

`OK Cherian, thank you for your efficient handling of the company affairs.'

` If we want, they will give us any amount as overdraft.'

`We don't require anything presently. Is there any auction during this month?'

`No sir, next month we can send two loads for auction.'

`What'll be our approximate monthly profit?'

`Roughly 2 lakhs per month.'

`Good, if we improve production, the profit will go up.'

`OK Sir.'

`Thank you Cherian. We have to discuss regarding a pilgrimage programme.'

`Thank you sir; I'll see you tomorrow.'

Cherian returned to his office and Rafeeque and Devaiah were left behind.

`Dewan sir, I want to go on a pilgrimage to Haj. I told this matter to the Maulvi here, but he don't know anybody in the Bangalore Haj House. Do you know anybody there?'

`Don't worry, you've to register for it now and wait for the allotment. I'll arrange the application forms and other details. I've some relatives in Bangalore.'

He immediately called his nephew Chinnappa and asked him to contact the Haj House and collect details. Next day, Devaiah came and told Rafeeque `you should go to Haj House and register for Haj today itself, otherwise you'll be excluded from the current year's list. Go in person and complete the formalities.'

Rafeeque immediately proceeded to Bangalore and completed the registration formalities. From there, he contacted his uncle Feroz and informed him about the Haj trip. Feroz was overjoyed and apprised him that his name will also be there, in the current year list since he had applied earlier.'

Feroz was accompanied by Rafeeque and they stayed one day, in the Haj House and flew to Jeddah together. After returning from there, he started to grow a beard and live as a true devotee of Allah. He sent a letter to Rabia asking her to resign her Job and return to India and take over the coffee estates. But, she declined and said `Daddy, I'm expecting a baby and he or she has to be brought up, decently. We've no idea to return to India in the near future after resigning our jobs. Here, we are safe and secured and no worry about future. We can't predict anything about our beloved India.' Rabia said.

`OK, beti your decision is correct. Live there peacefully; don't worry about daddy.'

Rafeeque called Devaiah to his bungalow and discussed some important matters.

`Devan sir, I 'm a grief stricken man now and fed up of life. I've done a lot of sins in my life and this may be the retribution. I want to dispose of my properties and go to Bangalore and engage in charity and humanitarian works. So many people are suffering in this world for want of money and care. Ever so many children are born in the street daily and become orphans. To wipe their tears, I'll devote my remaining life.' Rafeeque said.

`Rafeeque, I'll never approve of that .How can you live without anybody's help?'

`It is possible and I'll show you. You are living without your sons and daughter. My daughter will never come to take care of me. Nobody is indispensable, in this world.'

`No, Rafeeque, I'll never allow that'.

`Sir, there is nothing to worry about me. I 'm too much indebted to you. How can I repay the debt?'

`I've not done anything for you. It is you who inspired me to live. If you were not there, I would have become insane now.'

`Sir, I want to make a visit to Ajmer again and some other important places in North India. Are you ready?'

`Yes, ready.'

They went together to Agra first and visited Taj Mahal. He recalled the sad story of Mumtaz Mahal, Shajahan and his tragic daughter Jahanara, once again. From there, they went to Himachal Pradesh and spent two days, there. On the way back, they visited Ajmer and returned to Kotagiri. After reaching his bungalow, he gave an `ad ' in all leading dailies for the sale of his tea estate at Kotagiri and the two coffee estates at Virajpet and Hassan. Hundreds of bidders came in a short time. Only very few people quoted for tea estate and the amount in the bid was very low. The highest bid was from M/S Western Plantation Ltd and the amount quoted was only 5 crore .Since it is a job oriented industry people are afraid and reluctant to quote higher rates. For the coffee estates, there were many bidders including his uncle Feroz. The Hassan estate was sold to a planter and Advocate named Muthanna, Virajpet for an amount of 3 crores. He is a rich man and Ashiq is practising under him. He exchanged his Golden Valley estate with the Crescent Multi Speciality Hospital of his uncle Feroz, at Bangalore. Rafeeque started a destitute home near his hospital and decided to stay in a small room along with the homeless destitutes.

He met Devaiah and discussed the sale proceeds of coffee estates with him,

`Rafeeque the price of Hassan estate is reasonable. Adv. Muthanna is the boss of my son- in- law. The exchange of the Golden Valley estate with the hospital is really a loss. That estate is worth about 6 to 7 crores according to the present market value.'

`But sir, you are wrong. To have such a multi speciality hospital, in Bangalore city is not an easy thing. It is really worthy. I want to give that hospital to my daughter, Rabia.'

` To run a big hospital is a headache.'

`My uncle is fed up of this hospital and wants to breathe free air of Kodagu.'

`I'm not selling this estate and my decision is to hand over the same to you for a nominal amount. You register a company with your daughter and son- in- law and run it on lease, @ 8 lakhs per year. Proprietary concern is very risky. Income tax people will slap heavy tax on such firms, if it is proprietary. After one year, I'll hand over the same to your company, for a reasonable sum of Rs 1 crore.'

`It'll be a big loss to you and hence no need of transferring it to our firm. I've no objection and I'll act as you say.'

` When you become tired and unable to run it, hand over the same to Ashik. Let this be your share to your daughter.'

`Rafeeque, are you mad to give such a big estate to us for a nominal amount?'

`It is not free and I'll collect Rs 1 crore from you, later .You give it in lump -sum or instalments, according to your convenience.'

Devaiah was baffled and he looked at him with wonder and amazement.

The tea estate at Kotagiri was given on lease to Devaiah and Ashik, at a reasonable rate of Rupees eight lakhs, for one year, on condition that the same will be transferred to their name, after one year. A firm was registered with three partners Devaiah, Ashik and Preethy Ashik with equal share capital and Devaiah was made the Managing partner. Ashik stopped his practice and decided to shift his residence to the Estate Bungalow, with his mother and wife. Rafeeque prepared a Will in which the ownerships of the Crescent Hospital and the Destitute Home at Bangalore were given to his daughter Rabia, after his death, as her share. She can run the hospital when she returns to India. Rafeeque packed his belongings and waited for the arrival of Ashik and family. It was a clear afternoon and the weather was fine. A car pulled up to his bungalow and Ashik, Preethy, son Deepankuran and Krithika got down from the car. Rafeeque went up to the car and received them warmly. They were taken inside and entertained in the sitting room. By that time, Devaiah and his family came to the bungalow. Preethy spoke to his father, step-mother and step-brother. Rafeeque became gloomy. He was leaving his house once and for ever.

`Deepu who is your grandfather?' Rafeeque hugged the kid and asked.

`Which grandfather, paternal or maternal?'

`Maternal grandpa?'

`Devaiah '

`Will you call me grandpa?'

`Yes, Rafeeque grandpa '

Rafeeque hugged him again. He took out a 1000 rupee note from his pocket and gave it to Deepu. ` This is a gift from grandpa for buying sweets'

Deepu giggled in joy and ran to Krithika grandma with the money.

`Rafeeque, when are you moving to Bangalore?' Devaiah enquired.

`Dewan sir, now itself.'

`Why don't you engage a truck for transporting the luggage?'

`I've taken my dress and the documents and nothing else.'

`It is foolishness. You can shift the entire furniture and other things.'

`Dewan sir, I 'm going to live in a small room in the destitute home. I don't want any luxury items.'

`It is nothing but sainthood.'

`No, nothing like that. Simple life blended with self-imposed austerity.'

`In short you've decided to become a monk or sanyasi.'

`No sir, nothing like that. 'Rafeeque laughed.

Rafeeque started his car and waved his hand and then Ashik and Preethy went up to the car.

`I thank Ashik and Preethy for bringing your mother with you. It is not correct to leave her alone in that remote place. 'Rafeeque said.

`OK uncle, thank you for the love and affection, shown to our family.'

Rafeeque laughed and all others laughed in unison.

Rafeeque started the car, moved it slowly for some distance and then stopped abruptly; got down from the car and waved his hand at them. Devan, Deepu and Ashik waved back to him. Rafeeque got inside, started the car again, moved forward and within seconds disappeared from sight. Then, Devaiah and others moved inside and closed the front door behind them. Krithika peeped through the window and then a gush of chilly air rushed inside, caressed her cheeks and cooled the interior of the bungalow. At this time her grandson Deepu came forward and pulled grandma's sari and said `Grandma, why did you send that grandpa alone in this night.'

She hugged Deepu and sobbed silently.

---- END----